Time's Agent

ALSO BY BRENDA PEYNADO

The Rock Eaters

TIME'S AGENT

BRENDA PEYNADO

TOR PUBLISHING GROUP

NEW YORK

TIME'S AGENT

Cover art by Islenia Mil
Cover design by Christine Foltzer

A Tordotcom Book
Published by Tom Doherty Associates / Tor Publishing Group
120 Broadway
New York, NY 10271

www.torpublishinggroup.com

ISBN 978-1-250-85432-2 (ebook)
ISBN 978-1-250-85431-5 (trade paperback)

First Edition: 2024

For Soledad and Orion, for a world that opens for you

1

When the institute's dispatch hums to life on my old watch, I am in the middle of celebrating the morning of my thirty-eighth birthday. A frutero drone offers me a mango across my apartment's windowsill with its skinny legs. Supplicant position, I hold out my hands to receive it. The mango is dropped fat and heavy into my palms. It's an exorbitantly expensive new subspecies grown in PW 3751, owned by the United Future Fruit Company. My headlink chimes with the sound of the debit hitting my account, and then the drone buzzes away from my window toward the New Malecón. The mango rolls across my plate.

I crosshatch one golden slice, turn it inside out so it will splay. When I set that fire in PW 3751, the one that sent me into disgrace, it was in hopes that this mango and the others like it would never be produced. The literal fruit of my failure before me.

I stick a candle into the grid made by jutting mango pieces, a large paraffin candle made of petroleum by-product extracted from PW 7694 until its ecosystem collapsed under the oil spills coating everything in black. Another pocket world ecologically decimated, another update of the times. I light the candle, and it sputters and blazes the way I saw those mango fields go up in flames. Happy birthday, me.

Embrace the new times, I was told when I emerged from PW 3845—after forty years taken from me in the blink of a few seconds relative. I stumbled out of that PW into all that I'd lost in those forty years: the institute transformed, the entire world I knew scarred by war, my parents and daughter gone, nothing but my wife and the pocket world I wore around my neck as refuge. Well, look at me embracing it. No longer Agent Raquel Petra of the institute, but I'm still celebrating.

I am alone. Atalanta is crashed on the couch, rebooting. My wife has not yet emerged from the pocket world I wear around my neck; I haven't seen her for months. And who else would I even expect to join me? My parents and most of the people we knew in our youth just one relative year ago are now dead of old age or in the War of the Trees. Santo Domingo is a city I barely recognize as home; my apartment belongs to someone else. The sea rasps at the New Malecón just a few streets away, having swallowed most of my neighbors in its rising. The whole global institute reduced, brought to its knees, now at the beck and call of the corporations. Everything I spent my years at the institute preserving and researching now crumbled into ash or consumed.

I am ready to wish. I take a breath. The raging air in my lungs screaming to be let out, I chant, *I will not think about before, I will not think about before.*

But time never lets it be that easy, does it? Grief can make a single breath feel like a thousand years, but when you want to stay in the moment forever, time is a hound that hunts you down. Time, my enemy. Time, the thief.

2

We have always had stories of little girls who stumbled into other worlds, stories of children and adults and transportation vessels disappeared on hazy afternoons and moonless nights. Amelia Earhart. The ship transporting Queen Anacaona's captured husband to Spain. The Bermuda Triangle. Missing pirate ships and vanished flights. Fairies snatching children. Stories of time dilation. The stories of parents or children missing for decades, returned identical to when they had left. A son who just the day before had been a teenager with his whole life ahead of him, returned the next day as a bitter and broken old man. People returned to a world that had transformed for the worse. People who never returned at all.

And once we discovered pocket worlds and their door-points, we could enter and exit those other worlds at will. We could run tests, rationalize their mechanics, have debates in the scientific community about their origin. We could manipulate them. The first studied PW: one lone physicist in Buenos Aires noticed a prick in space in her lab that didn't follow the typical rules of thermodynamics. An entirely unrelated experiment that kept going awry alerted her to the doorpoint. In the aftermath of the news, she was tapped to create the Global Institute for the Scientific and Humanistic Study of Pocket Worlds.

The institute training manuals romanticized it, some poet hired as a tech writer having done the copy. I'm sure it's been rewritten since. "Walking along the sidewalk on a rainy dusk, the gossamer light catches an oil slick just so. Stepping into it, you are pulled inside. Running from the playground, determined to hide your tears in the woods, you fall finally against a tree trunk, let out your breath with a sob, and just like that, the day blinks out. Or the air conditioner shivers above your shoulders in your cubicle, the glare behind your glasses not from a computer screen, but from a strange pixel of light just beside you. You reach out, wanting something new in your tedium. Suddenly, you're not in the office anymore. Or at night, someone is after you; you're crashing through the back of a warehouse, running blindly with the acid knowledge that you're not going to get away, and then, you turn a corner and you do. You've found a pocket world."

It isn't always that simple. Most doors are wily. They have to be entered just so, or their positions in space are inaccessible. Their doorpoints are hidden or locked. Or you need equipment to bend physics, fluid dynamics, in your favor. And despite the poet's hopefulness, entering them isn't always an occasion for relief, especially with vast time dilations or inhabitable ecosystems. The poet never mentioned what awaits you inside, or after you escape. In some time dilations, spending just a single second in that PW means that by the time you come out, it's hundreds of years later in standard time, everyone you loved gone. In others, you can live an entire life and return to Earth Standard back to the second you left—except you are changed irrevocably. Too many lovers waylaid on their way to meet, families separated.

When we were young and still studying in Santo Domingo, Marlena and I would talk until late in the night about the pocket worlds we would discover, catalogue, theorize. Large worlds filled with astounding creatures for biologist Marlena. Pockets filled with Taino cave paintings and the palimpsests of cities for archaeologist me. Time dilations that challenged our understanding of biology or history. Back then, fools that we were, we daydreamed about going into a PW and coming out decades later, when it wouldn't be remarkable in our country for two women to love each other like we did. But we didn't know how the job would change us, or how the world would *really* change around us, in one blink.

As soon as we graduated from our PhDs in the States, of course we'd both applied for the institute. Pocket worlds had only just been discovered that decade. The world was lousy with hope for what we could do better. Every researcher wanted a job at the institute. The best and the brightest got in. Biologists like Marlena to study the new species we found in them, to theorize hominid development if it had been cut off from the rest of Earth, to study the effects of time dilation on the body. Archaeologists like me to catalogue the remains of cutoff civilizations, the passage of time on any evidence of human intrusion, to track the interruptions of history that had transpired by people moving in and out. Historians and sociologists to develop new theories of history and society that would allow for subjective time dilations and interruptions. Mathematicians and computational physicists to study the opening of the doorpoints, ways to enter, to lock them, and to pry them free. Ways to create them. And most important in the popular imagination: physicists searching for another full universe. Pocket worlds were usually tiny bubbles formed from our own reality, small derivatives of our own, penetrated by photons from our own sun. A rare few were as large as a continent. None were as large as the Earth, none their own universe with their own sun and their own galaxies. The only doors out we discovered came back to our world. But what could we do, given another universe, a do-over? So many people chased after the possibility of Universe Two.

Marlena and I asked to be stationed in the Santo Domingo lab, back home. Whenever a PW was discovered in the Dominican Republic, we took those engagements first rather than fly all over the way some of our teammates often did. Most researchers had their pet projects on the side. Marlena's Haitian roots gave her the idea to look for a lost storied medicinal plant used in vudu that she theorized had actually come from a pocket world. She also brought back cuttings, seeds and bulbs, cultivated strange new strains on the windowsills of our apartment. My pet project was the studying the Quisqueyan Tainos who history said had all been wiped out by Spanish slavery or disease. We knew so little about them. But genetic tests had shown that a significant portion of the country had Taino genetics. The conquistadors and sailors had arrived without women, had taken and raped Taino women. Any children who survived were subsumed into the conquistadors' project or slavery again, later having children with the African slaves and Arab indentured servants who were imported to take their dead parents' place. Mestizos, we Dominicans. I had some Taino, some African, some Indian, some Spanish in me, though I looked white enough to elicit comments over my green eyes and pale skin, enough to become a disappointment to my parents when I arrived from school with a Haitian-descended lover, prieta with unstraightened "pelo malo," and a woman at that. How far the golden child had fallen was their notion of it, and they screamed at me. After they stopped speaking to me, I replaced my parents' space in my life with my hobby project: I was determined that if any of the Taino had survived the Spanish by escaping into a pocket world, I would find them. Perhaps even a short-time world which would reveal them still alive the way they had been before the Spanish. What would it be like to talk to them? Would they claim me as one of their own, the way my parents no longer did? I dreamed up a brain scanner that would let me talk to the consciousnesses of even dead bodies.

In the glory days of the institute, when a new pocket world opened, it would be turned over to teams of institute researchers. Marlena and I would descend on a newly opened portal with our team, our grad student interns, our RoFido protectors, our equipment, and our research questions. We analyzed, catalogued, and preserved what was there. It felt like we were doing right in the world. It seemed like what we might find in pocket worlds would save us.

Of course Marlena and I wanted to raise a child. We were drunk with all we could do and discover. Our mistakes would never catch up to us, new discoveries always around the corner.

3

All it took was one step into a pocket world to bring me down. Those unhappy stories about families separated, the accidental touch that allows a portal to swallow you up? I have my own.

My birthday exactly one year relative ago. Thirty-seven. We were on assignment, and I was team lead. Marlena, Divya, and Isandro the intern jumped out of the institute van on a crowded street in Puerto Plata. One RoFido in front, keen metallic snout swiveling around to clear any threats, another whirring behind us to guard our backs. The crowd dispersed ahead of us with cries of "¡El instituto!" and then regathered behind us to watch.

We stopped in front of a crumbling colonial-era building, its cream plaster pocked where the stone showed through. Dispatch had told us a new doorpoint had been discovered there. A pizza shop had taken residence in it, installed incongruously modern glass doors, and painted signs advertising "¡Pizza y pasta!"

I looked up. Over the glass door, the key to its colonial stone arch looked different from the rest of the stones: off-color and carved along the edges, like it was made from a piece of something else and transplanted there. When I got closer, I noticed what looked like part of a Taino motif: an open mouth eating a Toa. Toa, the symbol for mother, carried a legend that a god had once stolen all the mothers of the island, only the men left, and the children had cried out, "¡Toa, toa!" for what they'd lost.

Report was that some kid had been seen jumping up to touch the stone after school, disappearing and reappearing to impress his friends, none of whom could jump as high. So that must have been where the doorpoint to the new PW was tethered. I launched my locksmith drone toward the spot with a flick of my wrist.

With the drone manipulating thermodynamics to hold the portal door open, Divya jumped up to touch the spot and entered first. Then Marlena, her curly ponytail and strong back disappearing in front of me. Isandro would be left behind with the second RoFido to work on untethering the doorpoint from the arch so we could bring it back to the lab. I reached up, ignoring the chatter of the crowd behind me, felt the grit of stone briefly under my fingers. And then I was in a new world.

I remember the meadow the way it looked when we first emerged from the doorpoint. A sea of lush green plants as tall as our chests waving and bowing like they were meant to receive us. Only our heads above the green. We let a cloud of drones loose around us, and they rose from the stalks like the pollen of new blooms. The buzz of insects worshiping flowers. The floral exhalation of the rustling wild. A small, burbling stream that cut through the meadow like a smile. The magnified curvature of the sky like we were walking through the meadow and the sky at once. We felt radiant, new, released from the crush of Earth Standard.

All our watches beeped; my first drone was reporting back the PW's stats. A small world, a little less than ten acres, and the dome of the sky above us curved heavily with the spherical distortion of small PWs. Short-time to the order of twenty, so we would only have an hour relative before the day in standard was done.

We worked fast in a happy delirium. Divya, star of the institute, had gotten a massive grant to look for Universe Two branching off derivative pocket worlds. Part of her research was estimating the breakpoint of the worlds we came upon, figuring out the exact point in time when they became unmoored from ours and grew the umbilical cords that would become their doorpoints. If she could pinpoint the conditions that created new pocket worlds, she might be able to create new ones or open new doors to the ones already here, even to another universe. She sat cross-legged in a patch of tender shoots and cohoba saplings at the top of a hill with her computers and sensors arrayed around her, lost in her work as her long fingers danced over her tech.

My drones reported back to me with possible archaeological sites in the meadow, places where amber might be preserved, where the density of the ground beneath might indicate former structures. It pointed me to a thick, cream-colored patch of orchids at the foot of a small hill. Heady with the perfume of flowers, I brought out my equipment and sent down a probe into the earth. Marlena criss-crossed the world, examining the botanical and insect samples that her drones tagged. Every time she emerged from the thicket to where I squatted by the orchid patch, she brushed the side of my arm with hers before she disappeared again into the green, and I shivered with contentment. I remember erupting into laughter when it began to rain—fat, warm drops that seemed ridiculous and plentiful, outsized in this small PW and its closed biosphere.

Isandro appeared in the meadow with a RoFido, calling for us, his boyishly flopped hair in disarray in the rain. He was about to untether the doorpoint. Even Isandro—who was just a grad student then, working on his PhD in computational physics, programming new fluid dynamics simulations for cracking PW locks—had settled into our team like he'd been there forever. He too was a golden child, already having written a paper proving that a rare side effect of two equal and opposite PWs—equal mass inside, opposite time dilations—was that their doorpoints could eat each other, creating a closed system, the doors never again accessible from our world. The discovery had rocked the PW scientific community for months.

A downpour drenched us. We yelled for each other to help throw tarps over the vulnerable equipment, and to stay dry we all jumped into a breakroom PW hung around the RoFido's neck. We crowded around a table in the breakroom's bunker, lit hurricane lamps. This PW was a small subterranean cave found with nothing of interest inside, and so the institute had remodeled it for our use. Its time dilation brought us approximately back to standard time as we waited out the rain, and the space distortion of small PWs magnified us all. The four of us laughed with each other, passing out towels to dry ourselves and bringing out old jokes in English.

Divya said, *Look,* and held her hands in front of her. She cupped the air as her watch beeped. A shimmering pocket of air appeared in front of her before stabilizing into invisibility. She stuck her hand in it up to her elbow, and we could see only her upper arm, the blood pulsing valiantly where it cut off, the bone and its marrow stark.

We all *ooohed* and I said, *Diache!* She must have figured out how to open a small unstable PW, how to stabilize the door so that she remained half in, half out.

Wait for it, she said, and from thin air she pulled out a cake tiered high with peaks of meringue along with cups of mabí. Everyone crowed and slapped me on the back. I hadn't told them it was my birthday, though Marlena bit back a smirk. Me, overflowing with a kind of grateful joy. This miracle that Divya had just performed. All of our

21

faces magnified and glowing from the candlelight, wavering with shadow. We were masters of time and space.

I didn't realize then that these were the glory days, that this hour in the breakroom would represent the fool's gold of my time at the institute. Earth Standard, with its overcrowding and hunger and political unrest? It might as well not have existed for us, except that Atalanta, our daughter, was waiting for Marlena and me back home.

What happiness we had then. We drank cups of mabí and danced merengue to our own hums. I laid my head on Marlena's shoulder as we swayed in the dizzying space distortion. And then Isandro cut in, dipped me deep over his bent arm, and I bumped my head on the table. I laughed as I fell. All of us happy and spent and just the slightest bit tipsy, collapsing on the floor. Isandro's wet hair on my stomach, Divya's perfect long fingers across my throat, Marlena's strong arms pinned underneath me like she'd tried to catch me. Laughing, untangling ourselves. All of our limbs curved softly around each other from the distortion. Then, somehow, the four of us were kissing, all of our heads together, more like we were kissing an idea than ourselves. I closed my eyes, smooth and chapped lips blending into one glorious triumph.

If you had asked me then, I would have told you that all of that would have lasted forever. The kiss. Marlena and I. Our team. Our family. The institute. Yes, there had already been alarm about the door to one of our largest PWs drifting close enough to the Ukrainian-Russian border, threatening to cross over, and escalating tensions over its ownership. There had been a few lone altercations caused by stray missiles or separatists even as far as Santo Domingo. But an institute team that specialized in portal tectonics had been deployed to that drifting doorpoint, and in that moment, nothing could touch us there in our nested world within world within world, like a chain of umbilical cords giving life.

I pulled myself up to the table from the nest of their arms. I made a wish I don't even remember now and blew out the candle flame still dancing on the cake, the breakroom's tiny pocket world spinning around me.

4

Later, we would be in a rush to get back to Atalanta. After the drone came into the breakroom to inform us that the rain had stopped, too much time had passed for us to do much before the workday was over, so we set the equipment to passive data-gathering in the meadow.

When we emerged into Earth Standard, the two RoFidos paced back and forth, holding back the crowd that had pressed in toward the doorpoint. Customers of the pizza shop ogled from the window. Isandro handed a small glass disk inscribed with the PW's designation to one of his drones. The drone flew up to the doorpoint, touched the disk to the stone, and transferred the tether. As team lead, I strung the glass disk around my neck for safekeeping.

I was still buoyed by happiness. As we left, I waved. People called to us, clamored forward as the RoFidos guarded us to the van. They reached for my neck, asked for money, asked what we had found. Some older children motioned the others back—likely institute hopefuls wanting to get noticed.

By the time we drove back to Santo Domingo, dropped Divya and Isandro at their hotel—our goodbyes still easy and soft with what had happened between us—and fought our way through traffic, Atalanta was already asleep. Marlena's mother had fed her dinner and tucked her in after the nanny left. My suegra gave me the required under-ear kiss, but other than informing us that we were late, she did not speak to me even to say happy birthday in her Dajabón-accented Spanish. She left the apartment in a wind. I knew she would be happier if I stepped into a PW and never came back—then, according to her, her daughter would be minus the lesbian seductress, her granddaughter minus the faux mother who didn't even share her biology. I'd learned to ignore her.

I prepared the initial team-lead report for the new PW until I gave a great sigh and took a break. Marlena stalked the apartment behind me, as amped up, sleepless, and world-lagged as I was, tending to her collection of extraterrestrial plants on the balcony, optimizing her aquaponics. The Malecón and the edge of the sea was still a mile away then, the sea roar covered by the night din of cars and people and the whir of hundreds of drones sent up by the delivery men on the street to people who opened their apartment windows for their dinners to fly in.

I hovered in the doorway to Atalanta's room. Atalanta's curls had sprung across the pillow, her breathing deep and calm. Her grandmother hadn't turned on the memory backup scanner, but she was too peaceful to disturb. My daughter, so beautiful and tender in her bed. I remembered the first time I held her, Marlena in the hospital bed crying at the birth she had just gone through, me with this vernix-coated creature in my hands, her big black eyes latched onto me even though most newborns can't keep focus, her hands already curling around my finger. She was born with a full crown of curly hair, and I kissed her head, inhaling the newborn musk. In that moment, I wanted everything for her, and I swore I wouldn't be like our parents, that I would let her change and be however she wanted. Years later, there I was looking down at her sleeping in her bed at six years old, all her baby fat gone and her gangly limbs at rest so rarely, pondering how quickly time passes. It was one of those moments when you recognize everything you have and feel full with it, while behind you, time the thief is grabbing for it all with snatching hands.

Atalanta flickered open her eyes. "What time are you now?" she said dreamily, remembering it was my birthday.

"I'm thirty-seven relative," I said, laughing at the funny way she put things. "And you're six relative and standard."

"Why am I the same in both?" she asked, sitting up now, her eyes alert.

"Because you haven't entered any time dilations yet," I reminded her. I cupped my hand to her soft cheek, and I sat on her bed. "But I have to go into pocket worlds for work, and they all have different time dilations. I've experienced thirty-seven years, but in standard time on Earth, some of those moments have been faster or slower."

"So what are you standard?"

"Hmm." I thought. "Almost thirty-five."

She settled back into her pillow. "Why are you always working?"

"I'm so sorry, pequeña. We'll celebrate with you tomorrow. Time was too fast. You know we have to get to PWs before anyone else can go in. Everything we look at is fragile and important."

She nodded. "I want to work for the institute when I grow up, too."

I felt something akin to sadness and pride mixed, a sharp squeeze in my chest at the idea of her growing up. Maybe even then I knew that everything would change, and not for the better.

"What would your research be?" I tickled her. "The search for the brightest crayon?"

"I'd go back in time to see the dinosaurs, and then to the future to meet the aliens, and then I'd bring one home to see my mamis."

I stopped myself before telling her that it didn't work that way, that time had so far only gone forward, that once you've gone forward you can never come back. A lesson I would learn myself soon enough. I thought, why puncture a wish so buoyant? She was as fragile as our smallest worlds.

"Can I do the memory cap tonight?" I asked, and she nodded, climbed into my arms.

I attached her scalp probes to the memory scanner and

turned on the dispatch comm on my watch because the voices often lulled her back to sleep. All that discovery, all those agents rushing to new PWs. Sometimes she would hear me and Marlena respond and be comforted.

I rocked her all the way down to sleep the way you're never supposed to do and set her between the blankets. She fell into gentle snores.

For the rest of the night, I dipped into the code for the memory backup prototype that I was using her memories to test. I had hopes that I'd fixed all the bugs this time, that tomorrow after she'd gone to school, when I rebooted her backup consciousness that had scanned and compiled while she was sleeping, her backup would speak to me in her voice. After that, I'd be able to test it on the mummies in the lab. If it worked, I'd be able to speak to the remnants. They would put my name on one of the aureate plaques in the institute headquarters in a dozen countries. I would be that much closer to finding out where all of our lost and broken histories had gone. I might even be able to speak to the Tainos.

Tomorrow. Such hubris I had then, one relative year ago.

5

Which brings me back to this birthday just a year relative later. One year after discovering the meadow world. One year after tucking her into bed for the last time. Thirty-eight.

To the rest of the world, I am a casualty of time dilation. Even the promise that I broke, telling Atalanta I would celebrate with her the next day, is a ghost. All of that so distant, so out of reach, I inhale over a candle stuck in a mango, ready to wish again. *Happy birthday to me. What time am I?*

My old watch crackles to life, spewing dispatch. I startle, let out my breath, the candle fluttering and dripping wax into the pulp but not extinguishing. I haven't turned the comm on since I was given a headlink and connected it to the new protocols. Atalanta, often comforted by the hum of the dispatch that she was listening to in her final human memory, must have turned it on before I rebooted her.

. . . Any available agents to respond. I know most teams are dealing with the explosion at PW 7657, but . . . First reports say some Taino remnants. Strange anomalies have informants talking about the big one. We're contracted to assist surveyors before the auctioneers accept bids.

Ah, the big one, the big white whale. Universe Two. What difference does it make who goes, just for a corporation to buy it, dictating the terms of humanity's new start? Better let it go to the dogs. I should turn the comm off this very moment. Yet the wish I've only half formed on my lips—that everything go back to the way it was years ago: the institute still in its heyday, employing the most brilliant minds of the era; me on the best team the institute had, preserving what we could, discovering all kinds of things about time and the universe, jumping from PW to PW trying to find new Edens, trying to guard the way there; and at the end of our stints arm in arm with Marlena and Atalanta—gets the better of me. I keep listening.

Agents call in with excuses. No one that I still remember from the old days. There are so few voices, I can count them on my hand, though back then we had hundreds, so many that only team leads were allowed to respond over comms. Now a skeleton crew stays on, the rest farmed out to the corporations or replaced by minimum-wage interns. *At the oil rig explosion in PW 85... At the nuclear waste containment of PW 371... This new one is located in Santo Domingo, isn't anyone close?*

Agent Alcantara's voice: *No agents available.*

Dispatch: *Everyone, this is urgent, we're talking about possible Universe Two here... What about our usual contractors? Interns? Who else is left?*

Me. In my city, too. But I am not on the list. I'm fired, my attitude no longer in step with what the institute has become four decades later, after the last big pocket war named the War of the Trees, after the First Step Act that gave corporations first dibs at worlds unless the institute could argue for a scientific or archaeological exception, after the institute's funding was slashed and the skeletal crew padded out with interns and contractors was run ragged. After I lost Atalanta. Me full of despair and a need to put right what has been broken. Lately I can't find anything that isn't broken.

The birthday candle burns down and snuffs out. I turn off my institute watch, put it in my pocket, contemplating the mango and my disgrace.

My eyes burn. I shove a gleaming orange slice in my mouth to distract myself. The pulp rolls on my tongue, bursting with a tang that reminds me of a floral rind I tasted on PW 2184 on break from a dig. Marlena had popped something in my mouth she'd collected from the weeds between the scaffolding holding open the earth. She laughed at the pleasure on my face. She told me it was a miniature apple, a new, almost citrus-flavored strain, one cultivated in a pocket world for a different time. She told me that centuries ago, imported bananas tasted different, but that particular cultivated species had been decimated by a fungus. The echoes of that flavor could still be found in the formulated candies that pretended

33

to be essence of banana. Essence of all that we'd lost.

As I chew on my birthday mango and the memory, my hands dripping with the juice of sorrow, a whir rises behind me, along with the *clink clink clink* of articulated body armor engaging. I turn to find Atalanta's irises opening as her body initiates. She works her metallic canine jaw into a stretch. I remember when she was warm and soft and she would melt into my shoulder on her way to bed.

"Preciosa," I say, wiping my hands on a napkin, extending my arms out to her so that the first thing she knows of this day is that I have come back to her.

She ducks under the table deftly, springs up to nuzzle my face as I hug her titanium flesh.

"What time are you?" she asks excitedly.

"Thirty-eight," I say, testing to see if the skipped year gives her pause.

She cranes her head up to me with an almost silent whirring of gears. "Where's Mamá?"

"She's still at work," I say. The lie doesn't even hurt anymore now that I've said it so many times. I rub my necklace, the small glass disk that contains the pocket world where Marlena retreated so many months ago.

"Come," I say. "We're going to the store."

She leaps, the apartment shaking as she lands. Her joy, at least, has never changed.

I do not remind her, as I would have done in our former

life, to put on her shoes. She follows me into the elevator stairwell.

"I'm wearing a costume," she says, her robotic paws flexing in front of her.

"Yes. I had to save you."

The autopilot of our old institute-issue van swerves and squeals around the parking garage to halt in front of us. State of the art, back then.

I help load her in the passenger seat. I order us to the Supermercado Bravo, ready to get out of my stupor and prepare dinner, a cake. Something to show Marlena that I'm surviving, worth fighting for even—if Marlena remembers it's my birthday, even though she did not come out for hers. Remembers that it's the anniversary of what happened to Atalanta. But aren't all anniversaries relative? We can celebrate and mourn every day if we want.

"Where are we?" Atalanta asks as the van weaves us through traffic, voice full of wonder instead of fear. The sea moved miles inland and now laps just a few streets away between crumbling buildings that collapsed when the sea overtook them. The streets are just as congested as ever, but now overhead is clouded by luxury Tiny Transports, mosquito drones ferrying short-time pocket worlds with passengers who will arrive at their destination in seconds relative. Working-class people sleep on the street in Portal Pod lockers in front of their workplaces, tiny worlds only big enough for a mat and someone to crawl into the fetal position, except most are too small and everywhere disembodied heads, arms, or legs jut into dodging traffic. People jump into the street out of thin air. Frutero drones call out recorded frutero songs from the beginning of the century, but instead of pulling donkey carts full of fruit collected from the outskirts of the city, now they lug retethered AgroWorld longtime PWs where farmers can indenture themselves for a year relative and come back the same day standard, before their kids even notice they left. Mangoes, bananas, cajuilitos solemán. You can lose your entire life that way, fifty years in just fifty days, working to feed the insatiable beast of humanity. Compared to Atalanta's last memory, decay is everywhere, and yet so much of the rot is invisible, tucked away into PWs, like the corporations have pocked the Earth into a pimply-faced teenager, deep pores waiting to erupt.

"A lot can happen overnight," I say.

"Did I go into short-time?" she asks excitedly. My baby, so quick. So attentive to time and the way it can efface us. She used to spend days running holograms of extinct hummingbirds on slow-motion, counting their wingbeats.

"Something like that," I say.

We turn the corner to the Bravo, and the autopilot brings us to a screeching stop. People pour into the ancient streets from a point in the air belching smoke. A pocket world burning. A crowd amasses in the street in front of the PW and they hold dismembered robot parts in the air. Some of them have set broken robots on strings with jetpacks and hold them floating, like a cross between balloons and lynchings, like hope and despair are twins.

"Get in the footwell," I tell Atalanta, trying to keep panic out of my voice. "Hide-and-seek time." We've played this game before, years ago, when I brought her to work once and people saw the institute van rolling down the street and mobbed the van, thinking they could stop us from arriving—though now, the van is cause for laughter instead of envy, a symbol of impotence. "Hush."

"I'm tired," she says.

I'm afraid to ask her the refrain from when she was human: *Do you feel tired here or here or here?* Pointing to my head, my heart, my stomach. Right now, I would point to all three.

"Can we go home now?" she says. "Is it time yet? Can we make it time yet?" Already she is a native of popping in and out of new possibilities.

"No, galletíca," I say, my hand on her metal back pushing her down. "We can't go home."

And because she's frozen at the age when nothing about the world makes sense, the age I perpetually keep her at with my resetting, she accepts what I've told her and curls up like a good girl to rest her head on her paws in the passenger footwell.

The chants are loud outside the van. Atalanta stays motionless below the seat, and I remember how much I still want to protect her from everything, from the world of hunger and need and hate.

I throw a blanket over her as we creep through the anti-metal protest, my hands gripping the steering wheel, hoping no one notices the blinking LEDs shining through holes in the knit. To them, she would look just like an outdated model of the robodogs the police use now, after the institute lost the patent to their RoFidos. A symbol of everything these people hated: metal and plastic taking meat jobs, metal taking resources, metal taking world space, metal easy to violence. That she has a human consciousness would be beside the point. No matter how many worlds we use and eat and expand into, there is never enough after the ruin. Never enough for our mouths and our bodies and our desires and each other. And how can I blame them? Once, I wanted so much, too. We wanted Atalanta to grow up surrounded by plenty, surrounded by love, a world drunk with its abundance. I was too lulled by our discoveries and the proliferation of new pocket worlds to think that it would catch up with us, our wanting, our need.

Hulking vehicles carrying construction 3D printers with a corporate logo emblazoned on their sides pull up behind me. Their autopilots honk at the stalled traffic like they are in a rush somewhere. Heading to the newly discovered PW I heard about on the comm, no doubt. Come tomorrow, these machines will be ready for the auction where the highest bidder will dictate what will be built in that world, what will be extracted, who will profit. The institute never even had a chance.

My foot careful on the gas, my van pushes the crowd aside gently; their anger surreal and open-mouthed, they part around me. Behind me, they climb on the 3D printers, using robot appendages to whale on any part of the machines they can reach. I'm so close now to the Bravo's parking garage, the entrance yawning open for me and a trio of guards playing at keeping the protests out.

"Mami," Atalanta says from the footwell. "I remember hands."

"Yes," I say, wincing, knowing what comes next, the litany of memories that means she is processing her reboot.

She tells me about her best friend that she had played with at the little L-shaped park on the Calle Jose Almanazar. What I know that she doesn't yet: that friend grew up into Pilota Primera Classe García Arcón, a decorated pilot for the War of the Trees, resting in the mass grave that is PW 494. The park finally succumbed to construction and a population that never abated. Apartments for the corporation execs stand there now. She tells me about passing near the obelisk on her way to school on the Avenida Winston Churchill. Now the obelisk's base is buried underwater and it juts out of the sea like an accusing finger. She tells me about the number of hummingbird wingbeats per minute, a bird she saw from her school window, and her school field trip to the botanical gardens just one relative week before, how the toucans opened their beaks to let out the most soaring noises.

I have heard this litany hundreds of times now. This consciousness I can't let go of. I listen carefully as I inch forward to the Bravo's parking garage, the clouds of transports and delivery drones obscuring its entrance.

It isn't until I slam my brakes at someone cutting me off that she breaks the memory dump, cranes her head up to look at me. "What did you save yesterday while you were gone?"

I swallow the lump in my throat. What did I save? Nothing. I couldn't even save her. She thinks I'm a hero, and I know now I never was.

6

One relative year before, the last day I would see Atalanta in the flesh, over the last breakfast we would ever have together, I puzzled over the PW necklace, over the fact that the doorpoint had been embedded in something that looked like a shard of a Taino carving, a toa, a frog, but the drone scans had disappointed me by not giving any evidence of human contact in the meadow world. Like the Tainos had refused to go inside or anointed it for the gods. A small little meadowland. That is what I was thinking about in the last moments I would ever spend with Marlena and Atalanta together, instead of taking hold of Marlena's hands, instead of reading a bug book to Atalanta over mangu and eggs like she wanted and squeezing them both until they yelled at me to stop.

As Marlena finished her breakfast, she told me she wanted to enter the meadow PW early. It was just turning dusk inside it, and she had a suspicion that one of the flower species she'd seen the day before bloomed only at dusk or night. She could have looked at the camera feeds later, but she wanted to see it for herself. A perk of being the wife of the team lead. She'd bring one of the RoFidos to test how one of the cahoba saplings reacted to different trample pressures on its root system.

She kissed Atalanta goodbye in our kitchen. Then she turned toward me with a dreamy smile, her hand outstretched in both a goodbye and a reach for the doorpoint. I loved her so much in that moment, her and my daughter, so much I could burst, but I didn't say anything. The last time I could, and I never said it. Marlena touched the glass disk at my throat, then the RoFido nosed it, and they disappeared.

~

I took Atalanta to school in the institute van, her giggling in the back with the two remaining RoFidos, who balanced over potholes by stretching their limbs out. I tucked her curls and waved from the van when I dropped her off. How much more would I have done if I had known what was coming? She grinned as she turned back to wave and skipped to her teacher, her movements still awkward with childhood.

As I drove to the mobile lab we'd set up in a room of the Ozama Fort in the Colonial Zone, I barely registered the news reports about the portal drift over the Ukraine border, tensions escalating, separatist terrorists taking hostages. I was insulated and happy. I was humming.

And because the autopilot was particularly efficient

that day and I would be too early to the lab, when an anonymous tip came over the dispatch about a PW just on the northern outskirts of the city, I thought I'd head over and take care of it before the rest of the team arrived.

7

I changed course, drove north of Santo Domingo, through a dirt road, down to a poisoned river. On the banks, a crowd was having one of those eviction sancochos, a celebration right before being evicted from their shacks by bulldozers to make way for new construction. A last hurrah. People danced merengue around a boom box in the road. Others were streaming out of their houses bearing the last of their food to throw into a giant sancocho pot. In went pumpkins, chicharrónes, slabs of boar, yautías and plátanos, yerbas. Centuries ago, these people would have been Tainos in palm-thatched bohios, but were now only their descendants mixed with their conquerors, mixed with slaves and indentured servants. Just decades ago, this land by the river would have been money-poor but rich with trees and animals. Now, the wooden shacks were crowded upon themselves right up to the edge of the water, and whatever the water touched, it poisoned. Someone was bathing their old motorcycle in that water, jeans soaked. Everyone was making such a ruckus that they didn't hear the institute van approaching until I was right up to the bank.

I parked, engaged a RoFido, who leapt from the back of the van to the edge of the crowd. The people scattered toward the shacks, giving me a wide berth, leaving just the two women who were stirring the giant sancocho pot and a group of people who stayed put underneath a thatched shelter as if they were protecting something.

I made my way toward them, holding my hands up in the air as if I meant them no harm. I suddenly felt foolish, having come without a team and with another pocket world vulnerable around my neck. Still, the two RoFidos whirred and marched beside me. I kept one hand in the metal ruff of one of them.

At the center of the cluster, a group of children passed around an almond-shaped object the size of their palms. It shone the red-gold color of guanín metal, which meant it was either Taino or a counterfeit tourist trinket. I guessed it was the artifact that the institute had been tipped off about, what dispatch had sent me here to recover. I tried to keep my face calm as the children threw the PW from one to the other. They were *playing* with it.

Then one of the adults shushed them. Someone turned the boom box off.

The boy who had most recently caught it looked up. "It's mine, I found it!" he said instinctively as I neared, and he clutched it to his chest. He was about six relative, the same age as Atalanta. Even in a defensive stance, he looked wide-eyed and tender. I wanted to cover his hands with mine, drape my arm around his shoulders, admonish him for holding it up to the light with so many people around. *Don't you know,* I wanted to say, *how dangerous it is to have anything of value—worth taking or discovering or entering?* The thought surprised me; I was not used to thinking that way since joining the institute. It brought me back to when Marlena and I first kissed and kept it secret, how terrified we'd been, our love behind closed doors.

I held up my institute badge. "Please be careful with that artifact. I have to take it with me."

"It's worth something," one of the adults said.

"And why should you have it?" another asked.

"I can pay the institute's standard PW-finding rate if it turns out to be a pocket world." I approached the boy slowly, my hands palm up. "I'm a researcher. I study them, make important discoveries that all of us can benefit from."

One of the women stirring the pot full of their last scraps of food harrumphed as she tended the final party of the neighborhood before they joined the mass migration of people moving elsewhere, giving their time up to companies, entering worlds where they could labor.

The little boy sprinted away from me. The RoFido lunged after him just as he threw the artifact to another of the children, who threw it to another.

"Stop!" I called. "You don't know if the doorpoint is open. You could fall in!"

But they kept running, the dog leaping for one then another, jumping up to intercept the artifact as it was thrown, a dangerous simulacrum of baseball.

The original boy caught it again near the edge of the river, his fingers curling around its shape, calling to his friends. And then just like that, he disappeared. The artifact dropped onto the bank of the river. Then I knew for certain it was a PW.

Adults started yelling, asking where he had gone. None of them would touch the artifact now. It sank like a blade into the mud, the poisoned water licking it.

A woman I assumed was the mother started wailing at me. "He was fine before you got here. You bring him back!" She pulled the artifact from the mud, and I held my breath.

The object, a guanín amulet shaped like an eye with a Taino spiral instead of pupil and iris, was now offered to me in the lattice cradle of her fingers. The dirty metal still bloomed bright in the smoggy sunlight. The part of me I hadn't yet realized was greed wondered if there were Tainos inside, if the boy was talking to them even now.

I backed away slightly. "How does the amulet feel?" I asked her.

"Ice cold," she said.

So I knew it was a short-time world, the energy of it chilling in its slow movement relative. I gave a command for a drone to deploy from the RoFido's forehead and enter the amulet. We had spare drones back then, a surplus that now would seem like glut. Back then, the drone was state of the art. Now it would be a child's toy. It flew toward the recklessly handled amulet, then winked out of sight. I waited while a crowd gathered.

"Señora," the boy's mother insisted. "Bring him back."

The boy could appear in a minute, or a few days, or a year. But I didn't dare enter yet. I would wait for the drone to send an initial report, and then I'd bring out a containment box from the van to hold it. I had so much to lose. My own family, my own little girl, what I had worked for at the institute. I had no intention of going in to save the boy.

What made me lean forward then, without the institute standard gloves, to the world offered up with open hands? Even though I knew better, knew that you could fall into a world with a loose lock, that some had dangerous or toxic biospheres, that time dilation itself could dislocate you from your life by returning you after everything and everyone you knew had died? Hubris, maybe, the feeling that we at the institute could do anything and it would be for the good. The assumption that we were the best and the brightest, and everything was better in our hands. That we were not using but discovering. I imagine, when Columbus first landed on the island of Quisqueya and was greeted with baskets of fruit, he felt the same.

I hadn't made a mistake in so long, not since grad school when I'd mishandled a PW full of dulled explosives and the lab head chewed me out about PW safety. As I stared at the amulet's iconography to inspect the spiral—Taino symbol for the immaterial, cosmic energy, unendingness—the guanín metal felt as bright as fire, a sun that could oversaturate, that could hold all of my brightest hopes. Transfixed, I thought about unendingness and the kiss from the previous day, how it felt that we'd all reached into each other. And, transfixed, I found myself squinting, leaning forward over the coin, the necklace holding the glass PW with my wife swinging forward from my neck.

That instant, I remembered Isandro's discovery about opposite-timed PWs eating each other's door, and instinct took over. I grabbed at the necklace to prevent them from banging together. In the process, my knuckles grazed the coin.

Horror struck me dumb as the landscape went dark.

I fell atop the boy who'd entered, the drone crushed between us, both of them having just arrived nanoseconds ago relative, the drone pinging my watch as it gave its entry report. "Short-time world to the order of—"

I didn't wait for it to finish. It was barely a second for me to register what had happened. That the world was so short-time that I'd entered before the drone had even begun to give its report. That the room I found myself in, lit by the drone's dim LEDs, was an empty subterranean cave, long since stripped of anything of value if it had ever held anything, though perhaps I'd missed the marauders just yesterday, relative. That I had fallen into it, and when I returned, nothing would ever be the same.

I swiveled back desperately behind me, hoping the lock was symmetrical, that out would be as easy as in. Hands waving, knuckles punching—only at the last moment did I hug the boy to me while we struggled.

8

I squinted my eyes against the flash of brightness.

We had been ejected onto the floor of a warehouse, hundreds of clear stabilizer crates and containment boxes haphazardly stacked and toppled in piles. Each held a glass orb, coin, stone, or fossil and displayed warning signs about the tethered PWs inside. The Taino amulet had fallen to the dusty floor in front of me, the acrylic box it had been packaged in busted open from our reemerged mass. The kind of life-wrecking short-time PW I'd always been warned about.

I fell to my knees sobbing. There was no hurry now. What was five minutes standard compared to what I was certain I had already lost?

The boy beside me. He looked so like Atalanta. My child I had given up for this one I hadn't even meant to save. "No. No, no, no," I wailed.

The boy watched me, perplexed. "Señora?" he said. He did not try to grab the disk again.

How could I tell him? Deliver the breaking of his life like everything I had believed in just a minute ago had been broken?

I saw faded institute logos and warning signs on the walls. I knew we were in one of the institute's warehouses in a section for quarantined PWs, those with time dilations too extreme or conditions too toxic to enter, ones where the drones kept not coming back. But the warehouses I had visited had been organized meticulously by institute librarians, the halls of neatly catalogued containers punctuated by labs where physicists pored over the most interesting PWs, prodding and submitting them to experiments. Instead, this warehouse looked leftover from an apocalypse. Dust caked on the floor and powdered my knees. Every third shelf or so had collapsed on top of crates and boxes that had then slid off to the floor. Some of them had busted open, leaving their tethered PWs exposed. Forgotten to the dust and entropy. At least the lights were on. The disaster of it distracted me from my own wailing.

But maybe—I had a flash of hope. There was still a chance that it hadn't been as much Earth Standard time as I had thought. As long as someone had realized what had happened quickly enough, sent the Taino amulet inside a long-time world to compensate for its short-time dilation. Maybe that explained the disaster of the place. If a few minutes in Earth Standard was a decade or more here, it would likely be years relative between anyone coming back here again to clean or repair.

I dragged the boy by the hand through the racks, looking for exit signs or someone who could tell me. I tried logging into dispatch with my watch, but it wouldn't sync, couldn't call out.

After walking through abandoned corridor after corridor, the boy beside me clinging to my shirt and whimpering, I finally found a guard sitting behind a desk in a little room, her uniform emblazoned with an unfamiliar logo for something called ALATechnico.

"Please," I begged. "How long has it been?"

She looked at me and the boy next to me, confused.

"I'm Agent Raquel Petra," I yelled, and then was instantly ashamed that I had. "I'm with the institute."

She shrugged. "So?"

I held my head in my hands. "Look, how do I call out?" I asked.

She ran her hands over her forehead and handed me a dot the size of a disk battery. "Where's your headlink?"

I pressed the flesh-colored dot, fumbled with it. "How do I use this?" I asked.

She sighed and attached it to my temple. I spoke the number I needed to dial out loud, but a voice thrumming in my temple said it had been disconnected.

"I'm trying to reach the institute," I told the guard, defeated.

She considered me. The boy trembled next to me. "Wait a moment. I'll call." She took back the headlink, placed it on her temple. Her eyes unfocused and I could tell she was doing something in her head. "You can have some coffee while you wait."

I almost screamed at her nonchalance.

The boy tugged at my shirt. "It's mine, I found it." Focused, like the rest of us, in the wrong direction.

"You're not in trouble," I told him. But I couldn't look at him. He started asking after his mother and his brother, and I kept my burning eyes toward the wall behind the guard. The company logo behind her was a nurse shark eating its own tail, devouring itself but with a smile like it didn't even notice.

After a few minutes, the guard said, "Someone's coming to collect you."

9

I wanted it to be my daughter, maybe grown up, angry at the abandonment, at how I'd failed her. Instead, it was someone from the institute. The man was no one I recognized, no fire bright in his eyes with the excitement of discovery, no fresh scent of wonder at the marvels in the pocket worlds he'd seen. A frumpy man wearing ill-fitting khakis and a harried tiredness. Agent Alcantara, he introduced himself.

"Well, well. Agent Petra," he said, like I was famous. "Time for a debrief."

The verdict: Marlena and I hadn't been seen for forty years. Atalanta, my love, my life that I had raised since the first days her eyes opened in the delivery room, had died within the week of our disappearance, casualty of one of the first military movements that would eventually be proxied into the War of the Trees. We never even had a chance to catch her alive. The boy's family had also died long since. They'd been drafted into the War of the Trees, most of them, the rest of them indenturing their years to one of the long-time farms.

Grief rose like a tide in me. I was drowning. My daughter. I willed my eyes to open, and then I kept staring at the shark logo. "What's the War of the Trees?"

I was too numb to register that the boy was being taken away by a newly arrived social worker. He hadn't cried once.

I reached for blame. "Why weren't we put into a long-time world to compensate? You must have realized what happened."

Anger on his face then and envy, which I didn't understand. Anger? And what was there about this tragedy to envy? "Yes, you were put in one, toward the end, even though the world rent comes out of our budget. That's what this is. But we didn't find the PW you were in until a few years ago. We just couldn't spare the agents to go looking about for a missing world without some kind of proven value, understand? And we still haven't figured out how to make time run backward." He chuckled ruefully, turned away from me to hide his face.

"Since when could we not spare the agents?" I said, shrieking in my despair, the feeling that if there had been salvation available, it should have been spared for me and Marlena, some of the institute's rising stars.

He whirled around. "You were part of it, you know. What's happened to us? I heard stories about those years at the institute, how glorious it all was. Well, now we get dregs. The companies take everything first, and once they've taken everything worth having, consumed all in sight, then we get to run our 'little experiments.' Even then we have to sell anything we discover or make back to the companies, because we haven't gotten grant funding in decades. And your fuckup started something. That mother wailing about her lost son, how the institute had taken him, how the institute was out to take everything from the people who'd rightly discovered the PWs and should be allowed to keep them, that's what started the movement. We didn't know that she was still hiding the PW from us so we wouldn't take it away and with it, her son. She said you'd pushed him in. She told the media that you'd left with the PW in hand, her son inside. Your van was found across the city. It was only after the mother died, decades later, that someone found the artifact hidden with her things. It only ended up in this warehouse after corporations decided there wasn't anything worth going in for. But before all of that, the media outcry, the government and politicians pulling funding, the slow-building perception that the institute was responsible for every lack in the world—that's on you."

"So why do you work for the institute?" I asked with bitterness.

"I'm not the best and brightest, señora. I barely graduated. I had no choice."

"My daughter's gone," I said, trying out the words on my lips.

"I'm sorry for your loss," he said. But he wasn't sorry; the words were as robotic as a habit.

"What would you even know about it?" I snarled, turning animal in my grief.

"Agent, you missed the war. So many gone. Whole PWs decimated." He parted his hands like a challenge.

I let all of this sink in. Ignored that soon I would have to be the messenger of all this tragedy to Marlena, who would emerge from the world around my neck, excited about a night bloom, confused about what had taken the team so long to join her.

Just as I thought it, Agent Alcantara asked about her.

"Is your wife still in the the mission PW? She disappeared along with you but the witnesses say they never saw her, and we never found that PW either."

I managed to get my wits about me and not touch my hand to the world hidden under my neckline, not call attention to it in any way, suddenly realizing that it could be taken away from me, that being with the institute no longer granted protector status. I suddenly understood the boy's wretched instinct to keep hold of what he wanted to be his. "No. I've lost them both."

I realized I had said "we" earlier and hadn't mentioned Marlena being lost, but it was true that Alcantara wasn't the best and brightest, because he didn't pick up on my conflicting story.

"I'll get home on my own," I said, hoping that I could before anyone saw Marlena emerge and guessed at what I had left to me.

"You have no home," he said.

Then I remembered. Atalanta's last backup, the one I thought I'd fixed all the bugs for. "My effects?"

He shrugged. "Those are probably stored somewhere."

"It's very important."

"Si señora," he said, and mock saluted. "But you should know, I'm technically your boss. I give the orders. You're still on the roster." He handed me a headlink like the one on his temple and the one the warehouse guard had let me borrow.

He paused for a moment, eyes looking to the side like he was paying attention to another world, and then he touched what looked like a mosquito and disappeared.

10

After he left, I realized I actually had no idea how to get home. The boy and the social worker had already left, blinked into the air. The guard was dreamily paying attention to something on her headlink. I sat on the floor, trapped. I had been in worlds smaller than this room, and they had never felt like coffins before now.

Finally, the guard got up to exit the room and screamed in surprise when she tripped on me.

"You're still here? Do you need help?" she asked, discomfited.

I held out my hands in helplessness. With a patronizing tediousness I had only ever heard reserved for the generation unused to PWs, she explained to me that the doorpoint at the front of the warehouse required force, no funding for a lock drone to stabilize it into touch-only. She gestured toward a point at the center of the shark logo on the wall.

I punched the doorpoint. I stumbled from a storefront into a busy street. I barely recognized El Conde, a street of tourist-trap souvenir shops and overpriced restaurants in my day, now with advertisements for privatized PWs pasted across the buildings, street criers holding out tickets and souvenir orbs, drones patrolling overhead.

I still didn't know how to use the dot Alcantara had put on my temple. I walked forward, avoiding eye contact with anyone who noticed me and lingered close, either to rob or to sell. I still wore my institute uniform, but no one flinched from me like they had just yesterday relative, like they didn't know what the badge on my chest meant or what it inspired.

I kept walking in a stupor, through what must have been the Zona Colonial and Gascue, until I found another street I recognized. Bewildering changes the years had wrought: half-limbs floated in the air as I headed down what was still the Avenida Máximo Gomez, what I would later learn were the coffin-sized sleeping-bunk PWs that were often too small for the occupant, their limbs hanging out into our world. Clouds of mosquitos around the cars and the motorcycles that blotted the sky to gray: small short-time PWs tethered to micro-drones, built for easy and relatively instantaneous commutes. Junk shops bordered the traffic, selling detritus worlds full of trash or poison, where intrepid scavengers could sometimes find something of value or use. Salesmen wandered through the self-automated traffic, begging the occupants to pause their cars to buy their wares, tiny purse worlds and pouch worlds and pocket worlds truly the size of pockets, and they cried out,

"Chiquitos, pequeños, bolsas!" to arrest attention. Department stores now selling fridge and cooler PWs, little short-time worlds that could keep your food cold for weeks, what just yesterday relative had seemed like such a miracle from Divya. Billboards advertising hand beauty treatments of short-time PWs stabilized with your hands in; I found out later that the more time you spent with them inside, the less your hands aged compared to the rest of you, with the side effect that the temporality-disconnect unsynced your nerves, and even with your hands out in standard, they tingled and numbed and didn't work well. Women with hands shaking like they had Parkinson's or walking around with hands invisible, they were "going to the beauty" as people called it. Every building, car, and T-shirt flashed company logos unfamiliar to me. I would find out later that corporations were mass-producing small pocket worlds with varying success, though they were unstable. At any moment, one of these worlds would collapse and spit everything inside back out to standard, and I could see the evidence of this as I walked, random piles of junk like a world had ejected its unwanted. I even saw one spew in front of me: a man skirting the edge of the road, ducking waving limbs that poked out into traffic, wearing chancletas and a loose T-shirt over his jeans, and suddenly electronics product boxes appeared, tumbling from his arms. Police drones zipped after him. Another woman walked by me, hunching, a lingering symptom of a recent chikungunya virus resurgence, and a trio of babies appeared in her arms. She nearly tripped over herself trying to catch them. Slow-triplets, I would later learn. This was childcare for those who had no better options: you could stick your children into a short-time cradle world while you worked, and they would be almost in stasis until you could tend to them again. You could tell when people used this method because their children would all seem to be the same age and never grow up and the parents would be ancient compared to their toddlers, because when were they not working? Time was now a commodity, easily manufactured, as easily thrown away.

I hadn't yet made sense of what I was seeing. Did this look like a world devastated by war? The only evidence I saw of it was a memorial in a rotunda of the Máximo Gomez that tourists gathered around, traffic speeding by. A metal forest of trees at the center, names inscribed into every leaf. Did this look like a world without Atalanta in it? No memorial to her, no evidence that she had ever laughed, breathed this air, begged to take home a street dog that ate a cookie from her hand. As for our parents, they were probably relieved when Marlena and I had disappeared, or maybe they had been torn by guilt, or maybe they remade their memories of us into what they wished we could have been. Everywhere I looked, though, the world was pocked with absence: the missing hands, the limbs without bodies, the sudden disappearances of people all across the street without even a lockpicking drone to issue warning. I kept walking because no one else was weeping, and when some tigres started following me to rob me, I turned around and screamed, my sorrow exploding out of me in guttural wails, and they scattered.

All of this as I walked in the direction of the apartment I had left just a few hours ago relative, dreading the moment that Marlena would appear in front of me, mapping the transformed city with my grief.

11

Our apartment building still stood, though the lower level was watermarked with previous flooding, the elevator stuck shut in a power outage, and the sea lapped just a few streets away. I climbed up the stairs hesitantly, hearing Alcantara's words echoing in my head. *You have no home.* Who would be living there now?

And yet, when I reached the seventh floor, our name was still next to the door number. I reached out my shaking hand with my keys. The lock turned easily.

Inside was exactly as we'd left it that morning relative, like someone had been maintaining the apartment in some kind of museum. There was evidence that Marlena's mother had combed through the apartment decades before. An old Bible and a crumbling wood rosary lay on the table by the couch. The dishes were cleaned, the beds made, all the perishables thrown away. Almost everything still worked—the stove, the lightbulbs—except for the TV projector, which made a grinding sound when I tried to lower it.

It didn't make sense. Entire generations had passed. There had been a war. We were gone. I slumped in the middle of the kitchen, the terrazzo tile cool as a time-dilated world. It was a mystery I couldn't bear to solve.

That's when Marlena and the RoFido she'd taken with her apparitioned from the PW around my neck, shoes and paws suddenly clacking on the tile. To her, it was like nothing had changed. Me in the kitchen, like I had barely moved from the moment she'd entered the meadow world, minutes ago relative, forty years ago standard. She didn't notice anything was wrong. She started chiding me about being late, briefing me excitedly about a flower, still budded, and a species of non-blooming plant, some medically promising enzymes excreted in its sap. She rested her fingertips on my crossed arms as she spoke.

How could I tell her?

"Marlena, go to the window."

Distractedly, mid-ramble, she looked out the glass. I knew better than to try to hold her as she realized. She went silent. "What is this?"

I told her everything, Atalanta's loss last.

"Is this a joke?" she said. She kept shaking her head, her curls dropping over her black eyes with the force of it.

I pointed my finger out the window, and she closed her eyes. I tried to hold her hands, to feel her fingertips again, but she shook me off and walked out the front door, the RoFido trailing her. Of course she blamed me. How could I have been so brash, so stupid?

I watched her make her way down the street from the

window, just a small figure. She sent the dog back when she saw the strange looks passersby gave it, and I turned away from the window to let it in the door after hearing its entrance request. By the time I went back to the windowsill, she was lost to the city. She wouldn't come back until nighttime.

I collapsed on the floor again, helpless. Then I pulled myself together enough to knock on a neighbor's door. A teenaged girl answered.

"Buenas. Can you show me how to use this?" I pointed to the dot at my temple. "And can you tell me who lives in that apartment?"

She shrugged. "A man comes by, but he leaves right after." With the exasperation that the youth reserve for the technically challenged, she instructed me on how to query my new headlink. She didn't ask me about my time disorientation.

Back in my apartment, I called the institute's new number, was finally connected after hours on hold like there was only one person at the call center. I was told that Marlena and I had accumulated two months' vacation, that the apartment had been sold to keep the institute afloat. "Do you have any idea what a whole apartment is worth these days?" the operator said.

"Who was it sold to? They don't live here."

"The old logs are kept on a warehouse server. Put in a ticket for the request, will you?" I got the feeling that if I did, I would never hear back.

After I hung up, I went into Atalanta's room, the RoFido following me. Everything of hers was almost where she'd left it just that morning relative. Her magnetic wooden sticks suspended in a half-built model of a stegosaurus skeleton. I'd helped her start building it when the institute had discovered a short-time PW with two mated dinosaurs, spared from the extinction event. Her stuffed mermaid dolls that she begged for after I described the moment we decided to have her: the PW with a minuscule sea, its doorpoint opening onto the jagged edge of a breezy cliff, below in the sea a small city of hominids who had evolved fish tails. Her tree house that modeled one of Marlena's PW discoveries: trees that grew into the shape of round houses, trunks giant and threaded from roots that reached up forty feet high, intertwined and ballooning out around a massive hollow. Though most of that species had petrified by the time we arrived, Marlena had brought back some of the saplings to pot and study. She grew one for Atalanta from a cutting, built her this living tree house. Now it had been tended, grown to the size of the whole wall. When it was still waist height, Atalanta and all the wonder that a six-year-old could summon, which was a world's worth, had set up all her stuffed animals inside the ballooned hollow. Once, she told us that no humans were allowed to live there, only the animals, because they would never cut it down, and we grinned at the quaint things she would say. Now, the smell of her was already forty years gone from the room. We would have no body to bury, nothing to put to rest except our shock and the feeling of grasping for emptiness. Of course, to Marlena, who had appeared in the same place this afternoon that she'd left that morning, believing what had happened was impossible.

And some of it didn't make sense. Why were all of Marlena's plants alive? Who had been here?

Atalanta's sleep recorder hard drive was still in her closet where I'd left it. I hadn't known what I was looking for until my hands brushed across the cool metal case. I held my breath for one dizzying moment.

One moment, I knew, was all it took to change a life.

12

I sat down on Atalanta's carefully made bed, the sleep recorder hard drive in my hands. Her last memories. My dreams of speaking to the Tainos paled in comparison to what I newly wanted from this box. The voice of my daughter. Everything she was. My arms around her. At first, I wanted a memorial, some vestige of her to lay to rest, to shock our brains into understanding that everything we'd understood about ourselves and our lives just that morning was over, had been over for a long time.

Then it occurred to me. What if I could upload her voice to my headlink, if this version of the programming had finally worked on her last night on Earth? I could have conversations with her until I was ready to let go. What would Marlena think? Me with my obsession with the dead past, her with her focus on new, blooming life. Surely she would understand what it meant to hear Atalanta speak again? I wouldn't have to tell her.

It was too much to hope for.

The robot dog had followed me to the bed, its gears whirring and winding. Queries about how it could help pierced my grief intermittently. I yelled at it to return to its dock.

I turned on the hard drive in my hands, heard the beep confirming its activation from the memory scanner on Atalanta's dresser. I closed my eyes and sent a series of commands to my headlink, trying to upload the prototype programming, but I wasn't familiar enough yet with the headlink's protocols to sync them. To my headlink, the prototype was ancient tech. So I didn't have anywhere yet to run the brain scan.

Then the RoFido returned to the bed, sensing my distress. Of course. I had based the head scanner's protocols off the language they'd used to program the RoFidos. They were from the same time and would be compatible. Before I could think, I spoke the series of commands out loud that would begin the data migration.

A few hours later, I heard Marlena return, the familiar sounds of her moving through our rooms, looking for me.

"I'm in here," I said.

The door opened. Her face was a storm. I couldn't find the words to tell her what I had done. I almost hoped it hadn't worked.

Then the RoFido, activated by the new motion in the room, bounded up to Marlena with metallic clacks against the tile floor. She put her paws on Marlena's chest and spoke to her in Atalanta's voice. "Buenas, Mamá," the dog said brightly.

I thought Marlena might cry tears of relief. Instead, she screamed. "That is not my daughter," Marlena yelled in despair, like she had been out looking for her daughter everywhere, and this was yet another trick the world was trying to pull on her.

"Please," I said. "You'll hurt her with those words."

Marlena was silent, hugging herself, not allowing me close. Atalanta asked what was wrong with Mamá. I stood by her because I could hold neither of them truly.

"Remember," I pleaded, "when she was first born? She was made out of you, not me, but I never let that get in the way of loving her, what she was made of. So maybe she's metal now. This can give her life."

Marlena stood up. "Don't tell anyone I've come back," she said. She extended her hand, her pale palm such a contrast to her dark skin. I thought she was reaching for me with some kind of forgiveness.

She touched my chest in a caress that hurt as much as a punch. Her fingers brushed the glass disk there, and then she blinked out of this world. The PW around my neck throbbed with chill, but no extra weight, as if she'd never even been here.

"Stay," I begged to the empty air.

I knew better than to follow her. When we had met in graduate school, she frequented long-time libraries, PWs where you could spend hours reading books or studying and return to almost the same second you had left, to give herself an edge on exams. It was how she wrote her dissertation on the potential of long-time worlds for the genetic mutation of certain plants and their human health symbiosis. When we'd had arguments while we were dating, we'd argue heatedly all the way down the street until she hit a sign marking the door to one of these long-time PWs, and then she'd reach out, disappear mid-yell, and come back after what for her had been hours' worth of stewing and calming down, and for me had only been a moment. The once I followed her was the once we came close to leaving each other.

I turned Atalanta off, reached for the dimple under her jaw, and rebooted her so the memory of one mother turning away wouldn't be the one that lingered.

13

For weeks, I fed my grief by scrutinizing history sites, articles on how and why the world had changed. The institute wasn't the only place brought to its knees. Entire countries ruined. Currencies and cryptocurrencies destabilized. The war heavy on everything. My own country's peso decimated again and again, tourism collapsed from trash and waste. Now the Dominican Republic's main resource was being a recycler of richer countries' trash. I marveled that just a few days before, I thought I had been above allegiances to country, when science had no borders or nation. I thought I worked for discovery's sake.

I went down to the parking garage on the lower floor of the apartment building on a lark. Somehow, the institute van I had driven that morning relative had returned to its space to rust, and it started up with a geriatric sputter.

I called the institute's new number again and followed up with my inquiry for who had bought the apartment. I was put on hold for hours. Too many hours of me alone with my own memories choking me. I hung up and called again and tried a different tack. I asked after all the people that I used to work with — people whom I'd laughed with, celebrated with, collaborated on grants with, cheered on when they'd been awarded. None of them remained with the institute. They had been headhunted by companies with more lucrative offers, recruited for war efforts, died in the war, died of old age relative in some long-time world where they'd been sent by new employers. A few had taken their discoveries and turned a profit. Divya had held on to her patent for generating tiny unstable worlds that collapsed randomly, building a small empire of PW fridges, Tiny Transports, beauty hand treatments, and other marvels. Isandro had taken his fluid dynamics simulations and patented the parallel processing hardware underneath them, and the mosquito clouds of Tiny Transports used his chips to fly together without colliding. He'd made a fortune on the war, using his chips in battle drones, using his software to train them into deadly patterns. A few of the others had stuck it out with the institute until their own bitter end. I followed all of these changes, keeping my mind on the causal links—the companies, the legal battles, the war strategy—like following it all could bring us back to a place of plenty. I felt like a beggar with a million hands held up and open and empty.

Most days, I lay immobile, paying extra debt for the delivery drones to come all the way through the open window to my bed, place food on my nightstand. My paycheck had resumed being deposited once I returned, but the rate hadn't kept up with inflation.

I didn't call the people I knew still left alive, ashamed of what both they and I had become. I hid from knocks on the door, and the doorbell buzzing of the dot at my temple. Ad drones haunted my window, selling years of corporate indenturehood in long-time worlds in exchange for the wiping clean of my growing debt.

Somehow, I could afford to grieve. For the moment, I still had the apartment and the RoFido that waited—powered down, chin on its paws—in the corner.

Weeks later standard, for Marlena a handful of days relative, she still had not come out.

14

It wasn't until I heard Agent Alcantara's voice on the other side of the door that I finally opened it. He had arrived in one of the Tiny Transports, which buzzed just over his shoulder like a large mosquito. He took one look at my state, wrinkled his nose at the smell of me.

"Are you surviving?" he asked. "Your vacation and bereavement days have run out."

I closed my eyes while they burned. Just a few months ago, I had felt open to so much, had kissed my whole team in celebration of what we could do and the glory of discovery, had kissed my daughter goodbye and marveled at her joy. I did not want to open myself to this man. I put my hand on my chest, hiding the glass disk with Marlena inside. A meadow inside. More than almost anyone in this world still had.

He waited awkwardly in the hallway, the transport alighting on his shoulder. "Look, no one would fault you for retiring."

I already knew that was a lie. He just wanted me gone. I should retire, get out while I could still hold on to my former life, even though just a few weeks ago relative my career had been spectacular and only rising. Except that I had nothing left. The institute was the first place Marlena and I had ever felt at home, felt welcomed into a family we made around ourselves. Now I was just a squatter in my former home, this apartment, and the person that had bought it might come knocking any day to reclaim it. We would need money, soon. All I had were objects that my loves had taken residence in. The robot dog, the glass pendant. And even those were stolen.

I shook my head.

"Well, then," he said. "Consider this getting called back into work."

He waited while I dressed, donning the institute badge and the rough clothes for an archaeological dig because Alcantara hadn't been wearing a uniform. Yes, perhaps digging I could excavate my life, I thought. I could return to the work that had sustained me. I kept my collar buttoned high to cover the glass disk.

He frowned at me when I came out. For a moment I thought he could tell I was hiding the PW.

He shook his head at the badge on my chest. "I wouldn't wear that. I'm not sure what things were like back then, but that doesn't mean what it did. The rest . . . will do." He looked away from my excavation clothes, and I realized he was wearing a plain polo and khakis, moccasins. Clothes for office work, clothes that back in my day would have screamed middle-class, white-collar worker begging for acceptance from some kind of corporate boss.

"What's the job?" I asked suspiciously.

"I'll explain when we get there," he said, and I could tell he was enjoying the withholding.

He reached up to his shoulder, touched the beak of the Tiny Transport. Then the space where he was hummed with emptiness. The transport hovered in the hallway, waiting for me.

I let out a breath. I could turn back into my apartment. Lie down, close my eyes. It would be so easy.

The transport chirped at me.

I stepped out into the hallway and closed the door behind me. I touched the transport's beak.

On the other side of the doorpoint was a small PW. Enough room for two seats knee-to-knee and the metal body around us. I had never been in a PW so small and the severe spherical distortion disoriented me. I had a hard time focusing on Agent Alcantara's face, which looked goggle-eyed and inflated. If the metal body around us hadn't been there, I knew I would have seen his face to all sides, like a circular mirror that just brought us back to each other.

I tried not to get transport sick, which I'd read could happen to some people from the distortion. I focused my eyes on my lap, where I held the badge I had unpinned from my shirt. I turned it over in my hands, traced its ridges. What did it mean to take it off? Another loss. Yes, it had been a home, a family. And my research, what I had thrown my life into uncovering. I wanted to make mummies whisper their secrets. I wanted to discover some pocket world of Taino civilization so that we could recover their language, know where we'd come from. I wanted to commune with them. I wanted to erase all this *progress* of colonialism and slavery and industrialization by walking through a doorpoint. Now it seemed all of my work was lost. Ancestors would stay silent. My country's indigenous past would disappear. Could I let it go along with everything else? Atalanta's human voice haunted me, *What did you save today, Mami?*

A timer beeped above our heads, telling us to exit. We had already commuted. I stretched out my hand to the doorpoint on the ceiling marked by an exit sign, following Alcantara through.

15

A rancid smell assaulted me. My headlink told me that I was in Jarabacoa, what I had known as a small town nestled in green upon green, threaded with waterfalls and rivers, a last refuge for people who had been driven out of the polluted coastal cities like Santo Domingo and Puerto Plata. Instead of that jungle- and waterfall-covered refuge, the concrete doorstep of a factory gaped before me. Around the building, trash billowed through the hot streets of a paved-over city and sent up smells of sulfur and rot. Lone flamboyáns punched through the concrete here and there. The street we were on advertised several recycling companies on the walls of 3D-printed factories. The street ended in a cliff overlooking a giant landfill of garbage. Towering apartment buildings rose up over the squat factories. Workers and robots surrounded the factory I stood in front of, shoveling trash onto conveyor belts from heaps that were replenished from thin air, the Tiny Transports in mosquito clouds above them dumping their loads. Land trucks came too down the road, carrying trash from poorer districts, people of all shades clinging to the sides of them.

I could see why so many people chose Tiny Transports

over land cars. There was so much you could avoid en
route. So much you could close your eyes to. I had read,
too, of people using the transports to evade la migra going
into Miami, their journeys almost invisible.

Agent Alcantara was already inside the factory behind
a sliding corrugated tin door, waving me into the relative
darkness. He'd likely been here for half an hour standard in
the seconds relative it took me to follow him through the
exit doorpoint.

The smell of the trash gagged me, and I brought my collar up to cover my nose.

Agent Alcantara did no such thing, held the door open
for me as I rushed inside, smiled a toothy wolf's grin like
there I went, the privileged spoiled child thinking she deserved better. Even in my grief, I hated him. He must have
chosen my first engagement to haze me, hoping I'd take
him up on the retirement offer.

It took a moment for my eyes to adjust. The air inside
was just as bad. Conveyor belts crisscrossed the floors of
the warehouse, bringing the trash from outside, terminat-
ing in what I guessed must be more doorpoints, workers
shoveling the extra that fell off the edges into the air until
it disappeared.

A manager suited up in bio-contamination gear shook Alcantara's hand and handed us our own suits to seal ourselves
up in. My hot breath fogged the plastic eye shield, but at least
the smell receded. Human workers looked at us warily as we

pushed through. My suit's plastic crinkled and swished as I walked through them. They weren't wearing suits.

In the old days, workers like this would have mobbed us as soon as we showed up, wanting some piece of what we had. Now, we didn't have any RoFidos prowling around us. The workers barely looked at us.

"Where's the rest of our team?" I asked.

"This is the team," he said, drawing a circle around himself and me with his finger. "We work in partners now," he said.

And then he explained the job to me. We weren't researchers, not anymore. We were cleanup crew and support staff. We had clients, were loaned out to companies whose funding kept the institute running. We went where we were paid to go. We closed worlds, usually, not opened them up, not studied them. We witnessed them, mourned what had happened to them, locked all the used-up worlds as best we knew how. That's what we were here to do: close.

This area of Jarabacoa was now known as a garbage processing neighborhood. This factory shoveled trash into a desolate long-time world where the material could break down over thousands of years relative. Most of the people in this region had indentured decades of their lives to a trash world the size of a giant landfill. Except even that landfill had filled. Then more factories had sprung up, stuffing individual trash bags' worth into small fabricated PWs, which held the trash—for a time—until they burst, spitting the trash back into Earth Standard. But by that time, the bags were elsewhere. People all over the world were paid to take on these garbage bags, these ticking time bombs of waste and poison. So many ways to be paid for your desperation.

Alcantara and I were here to seal off the landfill world, which had developed a mutating bacteria in one of the trash mounds that threatened to spill out into Earth Standard. The workers who lived there, erected their makeshift camps at the edges of the fill, had been infected. The infections had started that morning standard, two months ago relative. Already the first patients had died. Anyone left in there would be sealed inside. Alcantara and I—we were supposed to seal them inside. It would take weeks more for the bacteria to ravage through them all, for any survivors to realize they were trapped inside with no relief coming. To us standard, all of it would end in a day.

"For the good of the world, eh?" Alcantara mocked me.

I couldn't believe what I had just been told. Numbness took over.

The manager led us through the hectic maze of the warehouse floor, and I found myself following as if I were in a trance. Finally we reached the main doorpoint marked by an alarm and a flashing red light, and by the frenzied rush of workers trying to cram as much trash into the PW as they could before it was sealed, now that they didn't have to consider the human occupants inside who were being buried alive. Some robots cycled their arms in a blur faster than I could track.

"Hold this," Alcantara said when we reached the portal and all the workers stepped back. He held out a small watch-like machine he took off his wrist, and in my horror, I found my hand rising to take it.

Alcantara placed four hovering pegs around the doorpoint, and I realized I was holding what must have been the current iteration of the PW lock program, able to manipulate the fluid dynamics and physics of a doorpoint to gain entrance or scramble them to seal it. A large enough quantum computer could crack the lock, or someone with access to a data center in a long-time world that could spend generations of people to keep computers running for hundreds of years relative, spitting the answer back in a few minutes standard. My institute had had a quantum computer in its research labs in DC, but that had long been sold to keep the new institute afloat. Cracking locks required fortunes, and now the money paid us to seal, not open.

Alcantara vocalized a code to his headlink. The device in my hand beeped. In front of me, a certain heat and thrumming to the air winked out. Alcantara nodded. All gone, sealed from us: the garbage workers, the families they'd brought inside illegally so that they wouldn't be separated by time, the few doctors who had gone in pro bono to treat the sick.

It wasn't me who had pressed the metaphorical button. I hadn't been the one. I had just stood by. And this was the only certain quarantine solution to prevent the sickness from spreading further. What was I supposed to do? It had all been over in the time I had taken a breath to consider what I held in my hands. Even if I hadn't come on this engagement, Alcantara would have tapped another agent.

How could I stop what made this possible? I imagined some future archaeologist excavating Earth Standard, wondering what had happened here, displaying the findings in a museum the way we had displayed the remains of Aztec human sacrifices. What would Marlena and Atalanta say?

The manager led us back to the front, and my headlink pinged as he flicked encrypted ledgers to my data storage.

"We have more work to do," Alcantara said as we reached the tin door, roared it back across its sliders. His voice was a distant hum as he explained we had to audit the files, track all the individual garbage bags of PWs that had been contaminated with the bacteria, to bring back them and everyone who had handled them to be quarantined.

I pulled the suit's mask off outside, gasped, gulped the sick air. I felt bile rising up my throat.

Alcantara pushed me into the transport that buzzed into our faces. A minute later, I was home.

16

In my apartment, I had nothing left to me but my own tragedy. I couldn't bear to turn the RoFido on and hear her ask me what I had done. I couldn't eat over the stench of garbage that wouldn't get out of my nostrils. Instead, I threw myself into Alcantara's audit.

I pored over the accounts, traced trash bags to PWs to PW vendors to sales. I already knew it was hopeless. A quarter of the PWs had disappeared off the back of trucks. Someone had likely dumped the trash by the side of the road, hocked the PW itself as a larger than normal PW purse. Others had been sold to vendors who kept shoddy records, or no records at all. I sent my report to Alcantara. Recommendation: send labs inside long-time worlds to give them enough time to develop effective antibiotics. Someone would make money from the tragedy, I knew.

I looked at the time. Midnight. Already, no survivors left in that sealed PW.

I put my head in my hands over the kitchen table. I was alone with this. I wanted Marlena to come out, but it was a selfish want. I wanted her to bear part of this weight with me. Yes, there had always been tragedies around us before our time leap. But they had never touched me. I had never reached out to them. Even some of our old friends recoiling when they learned that I was novias with a prieta Haitian woman only stung from a distance; I had Marlena. I had been content with being an archaeologist and unearthing the past's sins from inside my kernel of joy. Now, I longed for the tinkle of bone artifacts falling into a jar from my hands.

I finally noticed a light blinking underneath me. The RoFido lay where I'd last powered it down underneath the table. It was low on battery, the indicator light strobing over my feet. I hadn't been able to touch it to either put it in solar mode or bring it to its charging station near the front entrance, could not—even tenderly—carry the body that had spoken to me in Atalanta's voice. I reached over, covered the little LED. But then my hand was on her head, warming the metal composite.

I brought my other hand under her chin. I needed there to be more to this life than closing worlds and the trash we'd made of ours and the detritus of better days. I pressed her power dimple.

Whir of her gears as she lifted her chin slowly. My chest constricted. How could I measure the time it took for her to look me in the eyes—these moments we are held so taut we could break, waiting for someone else? I held my breath for the length of a hope.

"Buenas, Mami!" the RoFido said brightly in her little-girl voice. "What have you saved today?" A refrain for every morning's greeting, a hero worship I now knew I didn't deserve.

How could I tell her what I had become a part of? "I'm so happy to see you," I said, a refrain that almost choked me.

"Please, Mami, won't you tell me? I'm a big girl now. You can tell me about your missions!" There were lots of things she had informed us she was big enough for over the years.

I walked to the bedroom, lay down on the bed, and closed my eyes.

"Please, Mami?" I felt her cold head nuzzling under my hand.

I kept my eyes shut because it was easier to lie that way. Finally, I told her a story. I told her about the trash world, but instead of sealing everyone up inside, instead of the trash I had tracked across the island, I told her about a garbage monster I battled back into the PW it came from. I almost cried with how easy it was to hide the ugliness of all of the worlds we had been born in, discovered, entered.

Marlena would have an even easier time of it, telling some version of the truth. Yes, she could talk about animals devouring each other, the way sap or stamen could lure or trap victims, but she could also describe the beauty of a single bloom, the trembling of a leaf in the breeze, describe the speed of a wing as the bird she discovered homed in on a pool of nectar. Was it because I had re-searched humans, and Marlena had researched the flora and fauna blind to our deceit? The point is, Marlena could have told her a beautiful story without it being a lie.

But Marlena had still not come out of the PW thrumming against my neck. I felt alone, even with Atalanta, her hopeful listening, her red battery indicator that strobed behind my eyelids. She tugged on my shirt with her mouth, her cool metal glancing my stomach, trying to pull me out of bed. I opened my eyes. (Why her mouth and not her paws, if she still thought she was a little girl? I only half paid attention to the thought at the time. I should have known even then that other programming was taking over.)

"Play with me, Mami?" she asked. Her indicator light had started blinking more rapidly; she was moments away from shutdown.

I couldn't bear it. "Run," I said. "Run, run, run." I leapt out of bed toward her charger. She pursued me, and then I heard a crash. I turned around to her splayed across the tile floor, battery dead, like I was witnessing the funeral I had missed.

What could I save? Not even her.

17

The next morning, when I heard the knock on my door, I was ready to open it screaming at Alcantara come to gloat. I flung the door open, my mouth already twisting into a rage.

It was a light-skinned woman with natural hair in the hallway, her hands in her pockets. She flinched. "Agent Petra?" she said awkwardly. "I asked to work with you."

"Why?" I said, through bared teeth.

Her shoulders climbed up to her neck defensively. "You're a legend."

I deflated. A legend. I was just the ghost of who I had wanted to be.

She peered around me, trying to see inside the apartment. "You and Agent Marlena Baptiste are both legends."

I stepped out, closed the door before she could see the RoFido, still institute property, behind me. "Tell me the assignment."

She started to explain, eyes wide and incredulous in some kind of misplaced hero worship as she spoke. She was young, I could see that now, couldn't have been more than barely out of university. Maybe she'd even grown up after the War of the Trees, had been raised inside a PW and had been born just yesterday standard.

I held up my hand. "Never mind, don't tell me." I would hold on to my ignorance for as long as I could.

~

This PW was on the coast on the Samaná Peninsula, known in my day for being the last bastion of pristine beaches, so coveted that a Dominican president had once tried to sell it for a fortune to the United States in the 1800s. An international travel company had built a resort around the PW's doorpoint, used the PW as an exclusive perk of the VIP package. When we exited the Tiny Transport, I could see the resort was part of a pump-and-dump scheme typical to tourism even in my day—use the place up without any maintenance or conservation, and when all the good is extracted, abandon the place to the locals. The concrete was decrepit with mold blooms and cracks in all of its palatial walls, the grounds were lined with sickly royal palms. Pink foreigners packed together in the lobby and stepped over each other on the beach. The smell of sweat and underarms and chemical sunscreen in a hot stew. The view of the water was smogged with a yellow sky. No one swam.

We pushed our way through the sea of people in the lobby, a sea I was accustomed to parting in reverence before me.

Blue tile mosaics depicting crabs riding sharks paved the road to the PW. At the center of the lobby, a sculpture of a mermaid with a gleaming crown and welcoming arms waited. The jewel in her crown was the doorpoint. A lock-picking drone in the shape of a barracuda held the doorpoint in open stasis. Other drones in the shape of fish swam across the ceiling. Half-naked Dominicans costumed with shells and tridents guarded the mermaid.

Once we flashed our badges from our pockets, the guards let us through and handed us oxygen masks. The mermaid queen's stone eyes judged me. I dropped my eyes before the sob caught for weeks in my throat escaped as we touched her crown. Then we were through.

18

On the other side of the door, a yellow sky just like the one we left. My breath was hot in the oxygen mask, my eyes pricked by something acrid. We stood on a cliff, a stone path under our feet leading to another hotel, abandoned, overlooking what must have once been clear water in a little cove. Now, trash covered the sea below, roiling like a skin of angry ants and battering the rocks. From the small crashing of the waves in the far distance, the curvature distortion as I looked out, and the hazy mirror vision of the same cliff I was standing on through the fog, I guessed the world was only a few kilometers wide. It felt eerily familiar.

I sucked in a breath and read the report of the PW and our assignment on my headlink. The erection of the PW hotel had displaced carbon-eating flora. Tourism had taxed the micro-ecosystem until it was uninhabitable. No oxygen to breathe, no seemingly indefatigable ocean to take the trash away. Now we were here to evacuate anyone left.

Why did I recognize this place? And then it hit me.

Our first job together when Marlena and I joined the institute was this cove. Vibrant with color, island plants verdant and rustling, the cove beneath inhabited by a mer species of hominid. Their vocal language was undeveloped, simple, just a few words like lower hominids, but their tails were as vibrant as koi fish, and they communicated with the subtlest gestures. I had been brought in to document the evidence of their civilization, rudimentary tools found on the sea floor made of mollusks, and excavate the bones of anything found on land to document the evolution from land to sea, decipher our common ancestors. Marlena studied the delicate ecosystem, how the merpeople were arch predators that kept the rest of it in balance. Their life cycles were long, but their gestations were long too, and each of them could only bring two or three pregnancies to term in their lifetime. There would always only be a few of them; the ecosystem couldn't handle any more. A linguist computer scientist was brought in to decrypt the expressive flicks of their tails.

It had been a paradise. Mer calls heard even on the shore, a sea as clear and turquoise and dancing with light as larimar stones, a reef that sheltered fish species we hadn't seen in hundreds of years and their new mutations. A cliff overlooking it all, where Marlena and I set up a tent while we researched, the linguist computer scientist in her own tent some meters away. The mer were friendly and beckoned us into the waves to bathe where they tickled us with the passing of their fins. Camping one night in this pocket world, Marlena and I decided we wanted to raise a child. We had seen wonders before, but in this PW we saw a group of mermaids surround a child and shepherd him through a ring in a coral reef, playing a game. He was the only child we had seen, and so it seemed like the whole tribe of them were dedicated to raising him, enveloping him in embraces and love. It was a childhood that Marlena and I envied, having been cast out or constricted so often by our own parents once they began to realize who we loved. Sitting on the cliff above the mer, I pointed with my lips below. "We could do that," I said. "That tenderness," Marlena said. We had fallen asleep under this sky, entwined. After Atalanta had been born, her first doll was fashioned after that merboy.

My headlink informed me about the hotel chain that had bought this world once the institute had been diminished, how tourists had choked the water and the air and the coral reefs had bleached, and the mer had been ravaged by sickness. The last merman had been saved as a tourist attraction in a large aquarium in the hotel lobby until the very end, where he screamed and fanned out his deep purple wispy tail to the size of the whole tank, until he died too. He was the merboy we had seen playing the game.

The new agent and I searched through the palatial VIP rooms of the hotel, overturning beds and checking bathrooms that used to drain into the sea and now backflowed brown water. We activated two drones to scan the water for signs of life, though one drone was so old that it kept throwing back error messages to our headlinks and restarting. Another two prowled the hotel rooms around us and their little red lasers jabbed across our path. I stayed away from the windows, the landscape view of what Marlena's and my hope had turned into. I sweated into my oxygen mask in the heat, felt like clawing it off my face. This time the engagement was to evacuate survivors. I told myself, if we found anyone, we'd be saving them.

It wasn't until we returned to the lobby and I had let out my breath that we found a survivor. One drone lasered at the dried-out old mermaid tank, where the last merman had died in a raging display. Mold clouds on the glass obscured our view inside to rocks hunched at the bottom. But the drone targeting it started an alarm blare, and scans of a human form were thrown into my headlink. What I had thought was a rock jumped up, shouting, clapping his hands to his ears.

A boy in a bellhop uniform and an oxygen mask. The other agent and I climbed up the tank ladder to pull him out. I'd later learn that he'd been born in this small PW, his mother one of the original cleaning staff when the hotel-within-a-hotel first opened. He'd barely ever been to standard, and he could speak the mermaids' now dead language by wearing a skirt over his uniform and flicking it just so.

The drones spotlighted his grief-stricken face and beeped in warning. He clutched the rocks at the bottom of the tank to his chest and buried his face in them, like he could be part of another Earth forever, a better Earth. As we pulled him out of the tank, he howled and clawed at our masks, waving his arms like furious tail flicks. His grief called to mine, and I wondered what that last merman had been to him.

We dragged him to the doorpoint. I wanted to scream with him, but instead I hugged him tight as he flailed. Then we were back in Earth Standard, security leading the boy away into the crowd, which roiled and closed over him. The other agent sent the barracuda drone the command to scramble the lock. The drone whirred and waved its fins. A sudden pop of heat in the air, and then the doorpoint was lost to us. Somewhere in the universe, that pocket world of poisoned waters remained, that world that could have been a paradise.

I turned back to catch a glimpse of the bellhop, but he was gone. I remembered the other boy who had fast-forwarded my ruination, the one I'd accidentally followed into that long-time world and saved when it should have been my daughter I'd kept with me. What was the boy's name again? What had happened to him?

As we walked back over the blue mosaic path through the lobby, I queried my headlink about him. The bellhop's face haunted me, and I had some idea that maybe I could help this other boy, that all of this was some kind of ruinous fate bringing us together.

Query came back: Alvaro Delatonio, who a few weeks

before had been that boy with a jutting chin, ideas about what was rightfully his, who had held in his cries and only trembled when he learned that he had been missing for forty standard years and his family had vanished in the blink of his relative eyes. Apparently, a few days after we emerged, he had contracted with a construction company in a long-time world, became an orphan in another land. He had already been there two months standard, which had aged him fourteen years relative.

I couldn't help him anymore; he was already a man. And what would I say to him, if I met him now? Me still freshly mourning, him with a wound that had cicatrized and gnarled over more than a decade? I doubted I would recognize him now.

When we entered the Tiny Transport, I closed my eyes rather than keep them steady through the distortion. The other agent put her hand on mine, so I put both arms around myself. When we had finished commuting, I closed my apartment door in her face.

Back at my kitchen table, I filled out the swamp of bureaucratic forms that had drowned the institute since I had left. The death of a world, dismembered into so many bureaucratic pieces—*exit population, atmosphere composition, biodiversity quotient, time of closing in ES, evacuation results*—that I couldn't even recognize what we had done, what anyone had done to it.

The RoFido's metal body was curled protectively in a

rectangle of sunlight coming in through the window, like somehow it was replicating Atalanta's pose when she was home sick and wanted to curl into our heat, laying her head just under my collarbone. I wanted more than anything to pretend, to step back into the life I'd left, for just a few minutes more. What was a few minutes more in the grand scheme of things?

I approached it, saw that it had fully charged off solar mode, pressed the button under her jaw quickly before I could stop myself.

"Buenas, Mami," she said. "Who did you save today?" She trotted to her room without waiting for my answer and jumped on her bed, where her stuffed merboy rested. It had been waiting for her touch for decades.

I remembered the bellhop's sobs as he was led away. Had I saved him? "I don't save anyone, mija," I said. "Not anymore."

"Yes, you do," she said, her faith in me blinding.

"No!" I said, grabbing her face to look at me with more force than I meant. She flinched.

I tried to explain, already pulling back, that yes, we were heroes once, all of us at the institute, but it was human greed, human want, that had conquered us over decades.

"Bad guys don't win," Atalanta said, petulant, because that was what we had told her in all of our stories. How simplistic.

I held her cold shoulders, found myself shaking them

as I explained. There were no bad guys. Or all of us were. Maybe more so because we hadn't thought we were. I thought I would explode with everything that had changed in the last few weeks. At some point while I spoke, I realized that I'd decided to reboot her so that today would be erased, that none of this would stick, so I told her everything that had happened, explained her own death and time and war and loss and love and how much everyone needed, and how even as an archaeologist I had found evidence of this in broken pottery, records of war and gods come to punish and starve. We both sobbed, her robot body shaking.

Suddenly she stopped crying. I was lying in her bed next to her and she stood up, her head lower than the rest of her and her shoulders taut, almost in the attack position of the robot dog's programming.

I wondered if she would put me out of my misery. The PW around my neck cold as guilt. I didn't move to defend myself. "Do you understand?" I asked.

"Yes, Mami," she said, but it was no longer Atalanta. Her voice was back to the dog's harsh intonation, and she was calm. The institute programming, protective, had somehow fused with her memories.

I reached up quickly to shut her off, sent the reset command from my headlink, my heart pounding. Horrified at what I had done, how selfish I had been in relieving myself of the truth.

19

The next day, Alcantara showed up at my door. "You could make this easier if you were on dispatch and we wouldn't have to come collect you."

But how could I? Hear the recital of worlds upon worlds dying? *Agents called to PW 3409, MPW 23, PW 987.* Skeleton crew that we were, only thirty of us across the world, entire countries we no longer operated in. Calling in contractors to botch things up when we couldn't. PWs that back when the world had been dazzling, when we had been so lush with plenty that I hadn't even bothered to learn their names. Now, I would let whatever assigned partner drag me into the next engagement, but no further.

So Alcantara dragged me in. This time we were in a transport for a few seconds, long enough for him, goggle-eyed from the spherical distortion, to stare at my chest where my badge used to be, like he could see through my shirt to the PW I had hidden inside, and worse, like he could see some black heart of me.

"This one's an easy one," he said. "We've been hired to report on the feasibility of an agricultural PW's ecosystem survival."

He straightened my collar, swiping my neck with his fingertips, and a sharp prickle of alarm rang across my skin in every one of my pores. I couldn't touch the exit door-point fast enough.

This time we arrived at a fruit distribution and packaging center, mangoes and apples and oranges painted on the external gates. Inside the courtyard, conveyor belts loaded and unloaded boxes from automated trucks and flying transports. Clouds of fly-sized shipping transports hovered above, mixing with the real flies feasting on fermented and rotted fruit.

I felt a ping at my temple as I waited for the Tiny Transport's time dilation to spit Alcantara out. An updated engagement brief arrived over headlink. Though the original engagement—before we had entered the transport a few minutes ago relative, hours ago standard—had been to put together a report, a few months relative had passed in the PW and the political situation had changed. We were now back in closing mode, except this time it was over political turmoil—strikes, labor agitation, people burning the crops and threatening to do more. We were still to do our report, but off different parameters: the cost of sealing it for decades. If it would be profitable, we were supposed to seal the people inside.

Alcantara appeared next to me, an amused smile playing on his lips.

I yelled over the shouts of vendors in the market next

to us. "Quarantining is one thing, but since when did the institute get involved in politics and strikes?"

"I thought you were supposed to be a genius," Alcantara said. "The institute has always been involved in politics. What do you think the things you made were used for? But now even someone like you can see it. None of us are above it."

"I won't do it," I said.

"That's fine," he said. That wolf grin. "You just write a little report."

An employee led us through the hectic fruit market, a maze of vendors holding tickets and yelling their prices over a paved concrete lot. He wore a logo on his shirt from one of the larger fruit companies I'd seen advertised all over Santo Domingo that first day I'd emerged. I'd drank their orange juice just that morning. Across the market, crates of fruit appeared in front of door-points and were hauled over to stacks awaiting transports and land trucks. Some poorer street vendors waited with their carts still hauled by horses and donkeys, though in the bed of their carts they had delivery drones. Some of the drones were outfitted with tethered doorpoints, their own agro PWs. I imagined that some of the vendors were hauling their own laboring families in there, bent over fields. They were selling crates back to the bigger companies. The fruit would go out across the country, across the world, in shipping boxes to supermarkets and people's windows on vendor drones.

The employee pointed forward. A drone's laser marked a doorpoint over boxes of green and heavy mangoes. We walked through, hands outstretched.

20

Inside, the fields were aflame and the distorted sky streaked with plumes of ash. This world was only twenty acres, all of it burning. This was a long-time world where people could indenture themselves for years relative, then come back the same day standard they left, their debts paid off. I coughed on the smoke before an oxygen mask wrapped around my face. I lost sight of the mapping and analysis drones.

In the seconds I had walked through the market, I'd downloaded a report on this PW. Another world I barely recognized. When Marlena and I had first discovered it, it was a swamp world home to a particularly ageless species of turtle. After the corporations took over, the rich land had been drained and set in strict rows that now burned in flame and ash, the turtles long poached for food and research on cosmetic aging enhancements.

Now, the workers' complaints ranged from a wage that was lower than anything they could have gotten in standard, inhumane living conditions, their own waste that they had to use for fertilizer, clean water rationed so that they often drank from wells contaminated with sewage, a plague of this PW's unique insect ecosystem now that the turtles who had eaten the insects had gone extinct, the pesticides they used cutting many of the workers' life spans in half, that they couldn't break their contract before their indenture was up, and no medical attention given. The many complaints of labor, that it used you until you were a husk, that there was no pursuit of happiness inside its walls, that it consumed time like a desperate maw, and that the rest of us, the ones paid living wages, in pursuits that brought us joy, ignored the cost of what fed us. We were there to stop them, and they wanted to stop us.

Crowds ran along the rows and gathered a few hundred meters away from the doorpoint, held back by the fruit company's private security force. Picket signs cobbled out of bleached, dried plantain leaves and mud that said things like LA HUELGA NO DA and ESTAMOS MURIENDO were held aloft and also set ablaze. People screamed, but not out of fear—out of anger. The same despair I could have seen countless times before if I had gone looking, if instead of the discovery of ancient remnants in pocket worlds, I had tried to see hunger and need standard.

The crowds surged forward, pushing security back, aiming toward me and Alcantara and the glimmering doorpoint. They looked like they wanted to burn down the standard world if they could get there. Dominicans and other indentured threw Molotov cocktails over the guards' heads. *Thirty percent complete,* the mapping and analysis drone reported to my headlink. Would anything of this world survive the inferno?

As I watched the riot coming closer, a bottle landed at my feet in the plowed dirt but did not break, the rag wick flickering against the ground. Atalanta's voice: *Who did you save today?* It would be so easy to touch the wick to my mask, the oxygen pumped into my nose the very thing that would undo me. The PW with Marlena throbbed at my neck, something else I was burdened to protect.

Sixty percent complete.

I picked the bottle up, the heat excruciating in my hand, the flame sputtering and flapping about. Then I launched it away from me. It arced through the air, the flame at its tip loudly roaring, until it reached the line of private security, setting a new blaze that roared at their feet. One of them caught fire on his uniform, pulled away to snuff it out. The crowd surged through the gap in the line. They ran for the doorpoint.

Alcantara grabbed me by the shirt, pulled me back through to Earth Standard as the drones came flying back: *Hundred percent complete: profitable for closure.* We landed on the market floor, the smell of smoke nauseating as I ripped off my mask.

I yelled and lurched for the glimmering point, but Alcantara pushed me back down as the lock drone whirred. He threw me inside the cab of a taxi Tiny Transport and then followed. Immediately, he pushed me out again, and we found ourselves in the same place we'd left, some hours standard later.

Stragglers in the fruit market were packing up their crates and carts, and burros brayed as they were hitched. The sky darkened with star-smothering smog. The doorpoint was gone. The lock drone hovered in front of us. The PW was sealed.

Alcantara pushed me against discarded crates of rotted fruit. "You have an attitude problem. You almost ruined everything, again. *Again.* Why can't you just stay out of the way? Why can't you just retire? Haven't you done enough to remake this world in your short life?"

He had ripped the top button off my shirt, and I clutched it shut so he wouldn't see what I was hiding. I said nothing, held his gaze until he was the first to look away. I held my hand out for a transport and collapsed inside of it.

A few weeks later, mangoes grown in that burning world would show up again on the delivery lists. A new strain, derived from a PW species. Seven years relative after its sealing, the corporation would unlock it, new workers would be imported in to reseed the fields, churn the organic waste from the riots so long ago. Organic waste. The new mangoes tasted like golden suns.

Blink, and anything could be unseen. Blink, and time's entropy consumed any order you made or understood about the world. How had Marlena and I and the institute lasted for even as long as we had?

21

The rattle of a key turning in the lock woke me up. My first thought was that Alcantara was coming to retrieve me or arrest me. I lay in bed, pretending to be dead, knowing there was nothing to get out of bed for. I wouldn't do another engagement. I almost touched the PW at my neck in the pinching manner that would unlock it to disappear from this world again. But then there would be no one to protect the disc, no one to protect Atalanta's consciousness. Wasn't this my lot now, to protect what was left to me? Still, I kept my eyes closed and wished for death, like those missing forty years could catch up to me in an instant and I wouldn't have to live them.

Then I realized it wasn't Alcantara who was prowling around the apartment. This person was watering plants, cycling the air conditioners, rustling papers, kicking through the trash mess I had made, keys jingling as they moved. "Is someone here?" they asked the air.

The mystery owner of the apartment. I didn't think to be afraid. Did I have the strength to face them? Finally I rose out of bed, opened my eyes.

A man screamed. His mouth dropped open with disbelief, and he kept his hand over his heart like he was about to keel over.

There was something familiar about him, the flop of hair, despite the gray, the age. "Isandro Delgado?" I whispered.

He stared, the keys hanging limply in his hand. "But you're a ghost," he said.

I pulled myself out of bed, a feeling of shame rising hot toward my face. "I feel like one. I fell into a short-time world. An accident." I spread out my hands awkwardly. "Hello, I'm back."

"Welcome back?" he said. He sagged into a dining room seat. "Did someone tell you about . . . ?"

"Atalanta?" I could barely say her name.

"I lament your loss," he said.

A silence passed through us. We stared at each other, registered the effects of the last forty years. Age lines sagged his face with canyons. It was unspeakable pity reverberating between us, both for different losses. Me for what I'd missed, him for what he'd lived.

"Coño, I'd forgotten how young and beautiful we used to be," he said finally.

I crossed my arms and clutched my shirt closed. "So, *you* own our apartment?"

He looked embarrassed, shrugged in affirmation. "I kept it for you. I had a feeling you'd be back in my lifetime. Of course, it's yours if you want it. You know, I looked for a connection between the bombing and you and Marlena disappearing." His gaze narrowed. "I looked for you for so long."

My eyes burned with a relief that threatened to flood over me. Someone had looked. Maybe he could help me with Atalanta. "How have you been?" I asked.

"Oh, I could have fared better. Just— Wait. Do you remember, the day before you disappeared . . . ?"

The golden day before I stepped out of Earth Standard, my birthday inside the world that now threaded my neck, the field that waved and seemed to call our names, the distorted sun magnified to three times its size over our glowing heads, our shrieks of laughter when the rain fell, the surprise cake in the breakroom. Atalanta waiting for us at home. The watershed holding back everything that would come after. I nodded. How could I forget?

"Is Marlena back?" he asked.

"No," I said, with a note of finality I hoped wasn't true.

He held his breath as he said, "We all kissed."

I waited for what he meant. Yes, I remembered the kiss. Hope-drunk, light-filled. All of us so reckless and loose with our bounty.

"The four of us . . ." He stepped forward, his arms outstretched.

"Oh," I said, retreating. How could I not have realized? He'd been in love with all of us, his older colleagues, him just a genius intern then and we'd brought him into our light. "Oh, Isandro, don't do this. We were celebrating. We all lost ourselves for a moment. I'm so sorry."

He exhaled slowly, like a gasp he had held for half a life.

"Forty years, and you haven't let go?" I asked.

"It's one of those things that's always bothered me, a question without an answer. Now I don't even know what was so important about it." He feigned nonchalance, but I could hear the dangerously sharp edge of bitterness. "You just shocked me, is all."

I remembered what I'd read about him when I was first catching up to how the world had transformed. I changed the subject. "So. You made money off the war?"

"No," he said, stepping closer to me. "No, you don't get to say things like that. Not to me. I was the agent who looked for you. For years. Even when everyone else had given up and left the institute, I spent my own money looking for you. Years I held out before leaving, and by then I had almost nothing. So yes, I made money off the war. I was brilliant, and I'd made a mess of myself, and the war was hiring. It touched all of us. You weren't here for that. And look at you. You're just so untouched."

How much did he feel I owed him? Atalanta's robot body was curled in the corner of the room underneath a window, and I suddenly didn't want him to see it.

"Get out," I said. "Please leave the key."

He threw it on the dining table. "Don't worry, I won't keep the apartment. I'll work out the sale details with one of my secretaries." He slammed the door, and I saw on the external camera he stayed in the hallway for a long time before walking away.

When I was calm again, I messaged Alcantara, *I'm retiring.*

Too late, he messaged back. *You're fired.*

22

Then I was alone with myself in the living room, the cacophony of drones flying outside singing their recorded advertisements, the crash of the risen sea a few blocks away. I still reeked of fire from the agro PW, a reminder of the burning of the last of my old self, and yet I could still feel her, half-charred, rattling inside me.

"Marlena," I shouted, but of course she couldn't hear me.

A few of the drones outside trilled about Taino tourist replicas. I knew their wares: cheap plastic amulets painted red-bronze to look like guanín, wooden replicas of squatting and bug-eyed zemis, drums roughly hollowed out with hide stretched thin. I looked over to the cabinet across from the couch displaying the arrowheads that I'd let Atalanta keep after she hiked the base of the Pico Duarte with us, just a few months ago relative. She'd been so proud when she'd picked them from the dirt. "Look, Mami! I'm an archaeologist like you!" Back then, all I'd had to do was witness her.

This time, I didn't hesitate. I turned Atalanta on again with a quick flick.

"Good morning, Mami. Who did you save today?" Always, our morning refrain. I had tried to live up to her.

"I saved you," I said, but I didn't tell her how. I patted next to me. She hopped up, and I curled my body around her metallic one, hoping that the dog's sensors were enough to communicate the love of being held but not the meaning of me being collapsed around her. She laid her chin across my neck, and I could hear my own breathing in my throat, feel the PW disk pressing against me.

I stayed silent while she told me about the last day she remembered, her yesterday relative. Again, her friend and the park that had disappeared under development, ghosts of the city of Santo Domingo eating itself and the war eating the world.

She looked up at me in the middle of telling, and I braced myself. Her head whirred down again onto my neck, but now she was contemplative. "Mami," she said, "why am I not at school? Where's Mamá?"

"She's thinking you are the rarest flower in the world, preciosa." I squeezed her metal body with everything I had, like I could stop what was coming next.

"Why do I have paws now?" She stood up despite me clinging, then froze like she was reaching deep into her psyche.

She looked at me with expressionless eyes. Her voice changed. "It's been 14,709 days standard since I was last mentioned in the records. Your institute license has been revoked. We are in Earth Standard at relative zero . . ." She continued with all the data she now had access to, flipping easily between the personal and the global, like she was downloading the new state of the world. What would she see, if she looked hard enough? What would she realize about us?

I turned her off, closed my eyes along with hers, both of us rebooting.

23

After a few days of squalor, the bed surrounded by takeout trash, me spiraling uselessly about how to keep Atalanta intact, I finally decided to face the people I used to know—anyone except Isandro. I asked my headlink to call Divya. A bright AI secretary responded she was in a slow-time world and would take a while to receive a message.

"Yes, I'll leave a message," I said, and then left a rambling, nonsensical explanation of what had happened to me and Marlena, hinted at what I'd done to Atalanta, which I knew by now had become illegal in the intervening decades. Divya had come to Atalanta's birthday parties, had seen her grow. Surely she would help. I begged.

"Your message will take two months and fifteen days to arrive. Is this an acceptable time delay?"

"No," I said.

"Would you like to begin again?"

"Yes," I said desperately.

Finally I just sent *Please help*, with my signature, and hoped that would be enough to pull her back into standard.

For a week I called various other friends, other agents,

anyone leftover from the war, age, or time dilations. All of them shocked to see me, all of them changed, the conversations awkward, all of them promising vaguely that we should get together. Down the list of people I was less and less connected to, until finally I reached the people I'd only worked with once or twice, and the last woman squinted at me and said, "Who did you say you were, again?" None of them could help me.

I waited for another week, resisting the idea, but I knew that Isandro was the AI expert. Finally, I called him.

When his projection appeared, his arms were crossed. "I'm guessing you didn't call to chat about the good old days. Do you need a job? Connections? Money? As you noted, I have plenty."

I cringed. I rubbed my puffy eyes and composed myself. "Actually . . . do you remember the mind-state scanner that I'd gotten a grant to use on the mummies we'd found in PW 463?"

"Sure, of course. Genius work. Shame you didn't get it working before the anti-upload clauses they added to the treaty convention."

"Just out of curiosity, what would prevent a scanned mind-state from breaking out of its sandbox to access the functions of the other programs on the hardware?"

"From being self-aware, but not too self-aware? Crippling the intelligence?" He relaxed into the constraints of the problem like it was the old days again and we were hunched over drones and an archaeological dig splaying the earth open, spitballing ideas. "This is a theoretical problem, right?"

Of course I couldn't trust him. How much had everything changed, had he changed, since I'd been gone? And that feeling inside me that demanded for the world to go back to the way it used to be—what would it drive me to do? Drive him, if he had a similar desperation? "Yes, theoretical," I finally said.

"I'd have to know the hardware, how the programming language handles the stack, and a host of other parameters. And it would depend on the psyche, too. Every being, machine or human, has an imperative. Otherwise no action would be better than anything else; the consciousness wouldn't be able to act. So, I'd have to know the psyche's heuristic. Its hunger, if you will. For some, it would allow them to leave something unseen. For others, every discovery is worth having, worth seeing."

"But couldn't you alter it?"

"Yes, but you'd have to start with those initial parameters." His projection leaned closer to me. "Would you have stopped yourself, if there was something you could have uncovered?"

"There was still so much we left buried," I said.

"Not for lack of trying."

I fiddled with a Taino arrowhead in my hand. I didn't even realize I'd picked it up. I thought then of Marlena and her joy when she found a new bloom species, the little sigh of "aaah" she gave when she peeled back its petals with her gloved hands. How Atalanta was the same, but about simpler things. When we crosshatched a mango slice, flipped it inside out to splay the pieces, how she laughed the first time we did it. Of course she would always try to leap over her sandboxing.

"I've missed throwing around ideas," Isandro said. "I'm sorry about the last time I saw you. It was just the years hitting me all at once."

"The years hit me all at once," I echoed in a whisper.

"You know, a long time ago, I tried to make it work with Divya. Personally, professionally. We were researching how to stabilize her smaller worlds and make them bigger. We almost—" He broke off suddenly, closing his eyes. "Well. It didn't work out. A bit of the same problem. We wanted to be self-aware, but not enough. We didn't deserve what we were trying to do."

His eyes flickered left, like he was reading something or making eye contact with someone I couldn't see. "Why don't you send me the old program, whatever you have? I could hire you. Or buy the patent. I could put a whole team on it. Even if we can't make it work under current legislation aboveboard, the laws will change sometime. I can put you in one of our slow-time worlds and you can hop out in a few centuries. I'll set you up. You won't even have to see me; I'll probably be dead by then. If there's anything we can be sure of, it's that time can shift even the seas."

At that moment, the chill of the PW around my neck deepened, reminding me of what I carried. It recoiled slightly as it expelled something from its physics.

Marlena appeared in front of me, her dark skin super-imposed with Isandro's image, her face unreadable.

"Look," I said to Isandro. "It's been such a pleasure catching up. We should do it again sometime soon. Talk about all the people I used to know yesterday."

I disconnected.

24

"Oh, Mari," I said, and collapsed into her arms, which, while not outstretched, still received me. She softened, cradled me. She smelled like earth, like she'd been digging, and her defiantly kinky hair was damp, like she'd bathed in the meadow's small stream. I imagined her inside the PW bivouacking under a gloaming sky, surrounded by night blooms that closed up as soon as she could see them, while I had been outside for months. I felt infected with the same bitterness that had grown in everyone around me while I was gone. *You weren't here. You sat out the change.*

I pulled away. I wanted to start at the beginning, tell her everything I'd learned. Instead I handed her her own headlink. "Here."

"What's this?"

I placed it on her temple, helped her with her first query, like the neighbor girl had done for me. Out of all the things she could have asked for, she queried for takeout. A frutero drone tapped at our window, the smog puffing into our apartment when we threw open the glass, the sounds of the city invading. The drone's claw extended to us, offering us sapote shakes. I added an order of milkshake made from a rare species of soursop discovered in a PW. It tasted like forgiveness. Her gasp when she took her first suck: something surprising and magical and maybe enough to keep her here in standard.

"So, I'm ready to talk,'" she said between gulps.

I spread my palms out, like *I'm here* but stopping short of *I've been here.*

"I'm never going to blame you for an accident, okay?" she began.

"I blame me though," I said. "I do."

She looked away from me. "Have you held a funeral?"

"With whom? Almost no one we know is still alive, or they're people we hadn't wanted to know. The estranged cousins I had in Bayahibe that stopped speaking to us when we came out? Everything has already moved so far past what happened four decades ago."

"You mean there isn't a new crop of chuecas at the church thrilled to pray for anyone listed on Sunday mass intentions to save their soul?" Her efforts at a joke. We'd not been to mass since we came out and could stop pretending. Our parents had put us on those prayer lists for years, the whole church involved in their own public dance of shame and redemption. The institute, that feeling it gave us of reckless joy, of something new and wonderful just around the corner, had saved us in so many ways. A new family.

"So it's just you and me." Marlena went to the pantry

and lit a candle leftover from our brownout supplies. It occurred to me that the power hadn't gone out since I'd first gotten back, whereas before, the brownouts in Santo Domingo had been a regular occurrence. Which PW had sacrificed itself to bring us the miracle of continuous light? She placed the candle flickering and hesitant between the two of us on a dish.

The shadows wavered on my wife's face, the echo of Atalanta's, reminding me that nothing could be permanent, all of us carried away by the hours, lost in the changes. My wife the botanist creating new life, me the archaeologist trying to unearth what had happened to us. Both of us dug in the dirt, but for different reasons, I could see that now. Even in the heady intoxication of discovery in the institute's glory days, my wife had been more like Atalanta. I had wanted to recover the ancient, wanted my discoveries larger and larger, had the hubris to think I could discover an entire lost civilization of our Taino ancestors. Marlena's discoveries could be smaller: the size of a pollen pod, the soft down on a succulent, a new bloom, her gasp almost inaudible. She'd wanted to pass on the quietness of green things to our daughter, wanting to break the cycle of screaming and yelling from her own family, the same reason that she would escape into longtime rather than turn to me with an argument raging on her tongue. The shadows of the candle danced across her cheekbones. Even after our years of marriage, I could see her differently. I felt old suddenly, like those four decades were settling in my bones.

She held my hands, her fingernails half-mooned in dirt. "Let's honor the treasure we've lost." She meant Atalanta, our glorious girl, but how could she not mean our entire world?

Begin with Atalanta. "Atalanta Petra," I said. Named for running and stones. When Marlena was pregnant, we talked about how we wanted her to fly far and yet remain with us always.

I thought I heard her voice suddenly, a ghost talking to us from another time, "Mamá! Mami!"

But then I heard the clicking of her metallic claws on the tile, approaching us. Atalanta, the robot dog freshly re-booted, padded into the kitchen, her face level with ours and eyebrows inexpressive. "What did you save today?"

Marlena shrieked, startled as I was. "No," she said firmly. "Not that thing." She pulled her hands away.

Apparently, Atalanta could turn herself on in response to her name. Yet another way Atalanta's programming had stretched its boundaries, even after a reset. I put my hand protectively on her back while she looked eagerly from one of us to the other. "Not a thing. She has her memories. You sound just like our parents when they first threw us out, all that talk about how their real daughters were these Platonic ideals that somehow weren't the very real people in front of them."

"This is categorically different," Marlena said, scrunching her eyes shut. There she went with the word *categorical*, like instead of naming the taxonomies of fauna, she was investigating the taxonomy of my failure. "Our parents couldn't see us, the real us. This time it's you not seeing her. Our daughter is dead. This new thing is something else. You've given it her memories, and you're making it perform for you. You're being selfish. *You're* not seeing her." She thrust the burning candle at me and stood up.

She was going to leave me again. Atalanta had started crying tearless sobs.

"Let's talk about all the things you haven't seen," I said, and threw the manual for Marlena's headlink at her.

She pinched the PW around my neck, her grief newly raw, and it was me she was mourning. Then she disappeared, taking the manual with her.

"Please don't leave," I said, too late. Even if the sound could reach her inside, it would be so time-distorted into such a small prick of noise she'd never register it. And then I held Atalanta as I reset her and ended her suffering before the other programming could kick in.

Of course I was selfish. I had always been.

25

I had enough credit that I could rack up debt for about another year. Divya never responded. I never called Isandro back. In the days after Marlena's visit, I settled into a routine: delivery by drone, try to reprogram Atalanta again, switch her on to debug. I kept hoping that maybe it was about input. If nothing rocked her too much from the girl she had been, she could remain herself. And for a few hours in the morning, I would have her back. We would run through the same conversation every day, with small variations I tested on her. We would read books in her room while the smog-light glowed around us.

I found a conifer on a bookshelf that I recognized as a seed pod of the petrified trees that opened in the middle. Surely the seeds weren't still viable. But I held a match under it to simulate a forest fire, planted it with Atalanta watching, let her stick her nose in the dirt, engaging her sensors. A week later, a sprout emerged from the soil. Though Atalanta had been reset and didn't remember its planting, she still gasped at the new life. Yes, every day I could relive my guilt, my love.

But each day, there came a moment when the dissonance between what she saw and what she remembered triggered her to reach out of her sandbox programming. I could see the change: the second she got quiet, her legs trembling as she ran down her rabbit holes of access. And then she was both girl and dog, both all the hope of someone who thought her mothers could be heroes, the worlds saved, discovery lurking in every future, and someone who had access to files and files of all the ways we had failed.

Every day, I reset her. Perhaps Marlena was conducting a funeral in that meadow world, but I had my own memorials, my own eulogies to enact.

Only once did Marlena emerge again, while I was sleeping. When I awoke, the curtains whispered like a ghost had blown through. Later, I would discover from our joint account statement, its negative balance growing, that she had received a drone delivery from a hardware store. She had taken her hydroponics equipment. The sproutling which I had placed on the window was gone, as well as the tree house from Atalanta's room. They left me the way that every miracle of a myriad of worlds had—suddenly and with finality, like I'd never even deserved it.

26

One year relative from the moment I stepped out of that PW with forty years gone, it's my birthday again. Thirty-eight.

Which brings me back to why this birthday I celebrate alone, a candle in the middle of a mango grown in a world I tried to save. Why my hands are on the steering wheel of the old institute van, heading to the grocery store. Why Atalanta is hiding in the footwell of the van through an anti-AI protest with people yelling all through the street around us. Because today, I want to revisit a place that felt familiar so recently and then examine the contours of how even the grocery store has changed, how even something so simple will never return to me. I'm being selfish again. I'm lonely. I'm a balloon filled with the ghosts of everything that was mine just a year ago, full and hollow at the same time, so close to bursting.

The Supermercado Bravo rises over the traffic jam ahead of me. Around me, a great roil of human need. The anti-AI protest pushes up against the walls of the Bravo, people pounding on the concrete with metal arms they've dislocated. They know that inside, there are no human tellers, only AIs and the self-checkouts that had already re-placed the people forty standard ago.

Blurring with the protesters is a familiar sight: a line of out-of-work poor crowding the concrete entrance to the Bravo's subterranean garage, hollering their skills at any-one who enters. If you feel some nostalgia about being served by meat over metal, they can shop for you, load your groceries, guard your car from thieves. Forty stan-dard ago, I had barely noticed them when I walked into stores.

On the street, people call delivery drones to their vehi-cles while they wait in traffic. The drones descend through a cloud overhead of Tiny Transports. The drones hover like jellyfish, arms loaded with chargers of various sorts, unstable PW tokens, and fruits and food containers dan-gling down to outstretched hands. Motorcyclists weave through the gaps between the traffic and crowds. Children with quick hands slip through the jam to try to snatch de-liveries before they descend. A few of them climb the great corporate machines as they lumber to a standstill and pro-testers pound on the metal bodies.

"Mami?" Atalanta says from the footwell, her LEDs blinking too much for my comfort.

I remember I packed the memory scanner in case I have to reset her from its hard drive. "Hush, mi pequeña."

Next to me, a group of corporate suits celebrate in a limo following the machinery. Through the limo windows

I can see them as they toast themselves with champagne. Though I know by now that land-driving instead of taking a short-time transport is considered a habit of the poor, the luxury limo must be an exception. I'm sure they're already counting all the spoils of the new PW I heard declared over the radio, and I'm trying not to care. They're celebrating their advance guard of machines of extraction, the various bodies of metal driving in front of them, construction machines which will enter the PW and take anything of worth, transform everything else. I feel a pang in the old, burned part of me—for creating something new, for discovery that doesn't come at a cost.

One of the corporates catches eyes with me, and I glare back, the only thing I can do. Always from now on, every PW I visit, I will arrive after the corporates, after the pillage.

Why have I brought Atalanta and me out here? Look at that sky, tinged with yellow, clouds coral-colored like a furious sunset, the end of something only a foretelling of the next day. Look at this roil in the streets around me, how there's no way to stop our destruction, how even being alive is the poison of demise.

I'm tired. It makes me want to volunteer to labor in a long-time world, the rest of my life just a blink to standard, my heart catching up to outliving its usefulness.

And then one of the protesters, who has climbed on top of a corporate crane, waves around a black handheld like she is conducting the cloud of transports graying the sky. The protesters around her cheer. Some bystanders, when they see the black box, scream.

I understand the black box is a weapon. She raises it, presses the button.

27

I recoil, expecting a boom to roll through the crowd, my windshield to burst. Instead, around me there is a brief and stark silence. The grind and squeal of machinery and rumble of land cars stops dead.

Then a cacophony rises up again. The dull roar of human throats. Clouds of Tiny Transports falling from the sky with sharp rattles, pelting my van in a violent rain. People hold out ballcaps to catch the falling treasures. The people and goods inside the transports' PWs remain entirely oblivious to the destruction outside them.

Atalanta's LEDs are dark. I shake her. "Pequeña? Pequeña?"

She doesn't move, and I try not to let bile rise in my throat. This is what it would have been like to lose her for the first time. I scream.

The protest surges forward, flipping cars and beating anyone that has a whiff of the rich or the corporate. They stomp to crush fallen drones. Anger is ascendant on their faces, some deep maw inside of them opening just wide enough to devour. Wouldn't it be so easy to lose myself with them, to join them? I reach for my door handle.

A man pounds on my window glass.

"Get away!" I yell. I fling open my door to push the man away.

It's one of the corporates from the limo next to me, yelling over the crowd. "An EMP!" He points to the institute's logo on the side of the van. "You're the agent they sent us? Does this old thing have anything that wasn't wiped out?"

Everything in me wants to scream him away, join the angry crowd, stop his imposition into my pain. Then, I process what he's said. An EMP . . . That means Atalanta's memory is still intact, run off of non-electric solid state; it's just her power source that's fried. Fixable.

But then, as I stare at him, I realize I know him. Or a previous version of him: a little boy so invested in keeping what he had. A boy who lost everyone he'd loved when he fell into a PW with an institute agent on his heels. A hand that clung even as his arm pushed me away.

"Alvaro Delatonio?" I say. He looks the same age as me relative. I know he lived decades in a long-time world by the time I thought to look him up, so I shouldn't be as surprised as I am. The long-time world where he indentured himself was hard on him; now he has scars across his cheeks that give his dark forehead the look of a thundercloud releasing sheets of rain. He's clearly climbed up the corporate ladder, donning a humble guayabera under an ill-fitting suit.

He gawks, then both his hands pull his collar up to the

edge of his jaw. "Coño. It's you." The people around us shout and clamor.

"Look at you now," I say, bitterness hot on my tongue. This child, alive. My child, eaten by time.

He looks like a little boy again, angry and petulant, the thundercloud rippling across his face. He purses his lips in defiance, lifts his chin, like I'm here to judge what he's made of his life. He's had decades to figure out what I mean to him, to transform the minutes we had together as the pivotal spurring of his life. "You took so much," he says.

"Now you're the one taking worlds," I say, pointing to the corporate limo. A group of motorcyclists surge around us away from the protest. The crowd is almost to the van. If they find Atalanta's body, they'll drag her out.

"I can't believe they would send you." He smacks the door's logo so hard that it shuts.

"They didn't," I say through the door.

The old van's backup manual transmission is still engaged, unaffected by the EMP, and when I pound the gas in reverse, the tires jolt backward. I force the van back through a break in the line, following the motorcyclists. Delatonio kicks the hood of the van as it retreats from him.

I have to find somewhere safe to repair Atalanta. I look around the billboards and advertisements on the buildings for a PW where I can let all this pass me by. But then it occurs to me . . . with all the corporates frozen in traffic, this will be the only chance I will ever have again to arrive in a PW before a corporation hollows it out or repurposes it for use.

I tap my headlink. It buzzes, but luckily it's necessary enough tech that it was Faraday shielded in manufacturing. I hook it for the first time into the institute's dispatch. I announce, "This is Agent Raquel Petra. I'll take the new PW."

Acknowledged. The operator, relieved, gives me more details. The last known GPS location of the doorpoint. A long-time world to the order of twenty.

"Received." I can't help a coat of adrenaline prickling my skin. No team, not like before.

Agent Alcantara's voice: *Wait, did you say Agent Petra? You're fired. You can't—*

I disconnect dispatch from my audio feed. With a long-time portal, I might have hours, maybe half a day in there before they catch me. In front of me, Delatonio and the other corporates stream out of their limo, backing away from the frozen machines and the angry crowd, trying to stay ahead of the wave that comes for them. Maybe they, too, are starting to feel the turning of the same tide I ignored forty years ago, the end of their epoch of bounty. They start hailing motorcycles.

I have no plan except to beat them to the doorpoint and have time to restart Atalanta. Can Delatonio guess what I intend? I peel the van around from reverse into drive, my heart thumping in my rib cage, my charred self reviving into a scream with the wail of my engine.

28

My headlink projects a course to the GPS blip, close to a part of the old Malecón that hasn't been subsumed by the sea, a section where a housing slum covers the beach and extends out on stilts into the water. The van dodges limbs sticking out of cubby PWs too small for them, drones spilling into the streets hocking breathing masks for the smog. I speed through all the invisible people folded into space inside their pocket worlds, an entire set of other dimensions we have overrun. I head toward a street I used to know, a shortcut to the New Malecón, that's been flooded for decades standard with a few inches of creeping ocean. The corporate's motorcycles will have to go around, but my van splashes through. The van rolls solitary through the flooded street, the crumbling, waterlogged buildings only harboring occupants on their higher floors.

As I approach the Malecón, I can see out to the horizon, the piss-yellow sky, the thousands of tent dinghies, shacks on stilts, and rafts that mottle the coast with overflow humans hoping to get lucky and catch the last fish on Earth. Spider-robots scuttle across the sand trying to keep up with human waste both bodily and trash, picking between the people that bustle, collapse, or wash up on the beach. Drones fight over coconuts hanging in sickly palms. The GPS marker for the doorpoint blips across the beach through the throng.

I stop the van when I reach sand. I roll Atalanta over, insert a screwdriver in a small hole where her belly button should be, and eject her old power source manually. I grab another from the van's back Faraday box, insert it. I pull the decades-old supply suitcase from the back, everything needed for an institute team to survive three months in a long-time portal. I pull out the case with my old research scanner. I thank the old institute for having the foresight to shield the supply cases, though back then it was against unstable PWs and drones that could short-circuit while trying to unlock a doorpoint. I hear a small whir, and Atalanta begins her boot-up sequence.

I struggle under the load, the supply case in one hand, the scanner in the other. Atalanta's heavy body swings and droops over my arms, her paws twitching as she boots. I just have to make it to the doorpoint, I remind myself as my arms burn with weight.

The GPS leads me through the crowd, across the sand and rocks, to a cave that from one side looks like a small sand dune at the lip of the shore. I wade into the water, holding Atalanta and the cases above it, my arms trembling with near collapse as I pick around boats and people that nudge me from each side. From the water, I now can see the cave opening. The sea threads between the rafts and tent dinghies before slapping against the jutting rocks guarding the cave mouth. The cave must have only recently been unearthed by the drowning sea.

When I stand in the opening of the cave, my form casts long shadows over the people gathered inside. The clamor of humans echoes like a frenzied market.

"Policía!" I hear reverberating inside. I remember when people would call out as a warning, "The institute is here!" but now that phrase holds no power. Now, carrying my dead daughter in my arms looks to them like I'm police with a famously brutal police dog, come to enforce, to accept bribes, to give them fines they can only pay with indentured time.

The mouth of the cave starts spilling people into the water, some of them falling on hands and knees. I stumble as people plow into me, and I cling to Atalanta as I'm battered from side to side. They keep coming, thousands of them, more than that cave could ever contain if it didn't have a PW bending space-time inside. An elbow cracks me in the head, and I fall to my knees. Stomp after stomp on my legs, and I manage to hold on to what's in my arms as I drag myself behind the cave's opening. People push out into the water, overturn rafts, clamber onto dinghies and stilt houses, coat the shore. Around me looks like an ant mound when it's been disturbed: bodies covering the earth in an angry, crawling crust.

I catch my breath, wincing at the new bruises, keeping out of the way of the stampede, the layering upon layering of people indicative of a long-time world spitting out its former inhabitants into the same span of a few minutes, even though it probably took them an hour relative to return to the doorpoint after the initial warning of "Policía!" had been shouted.

Down the beach, I see Delatonio arrive on a motorcycle, the stampede rushing toward him leaving crushed bodies in their wake. The anti-AI protest is right behind him, chanting the name of his corporation. I have at most a ten-minute standard head start, which might give me a few hours inside. *Please wake up,* I beg Atalanta.

I send a message to Divya and Isandro with my headlink, begging them to come to the doorpoint. If our friendship meant anything all those decades for them ago, they'll come. Maybe they'll even get here in time to extract me from the mess I've gotten myself into.

I push forward into the crowded darkness of the cave, dragging Atalanta and the equipment cases while trying to protect my face against the rush of elbows, knees, and feet barraging in the other direction. The cave extends fifty meters, short stalactites punctuating the ceiling, stalagmites on the floor already trampled away to nubs. I track the sudden apparition of bodies to a small spot along the limestone wall, a Taino cave painting of a fish almost entirely rubbed away into a speck of red. Dodging what I hope is the last refugee fleeing the doorpoint, I throw myself at it, pulling Atalanta and my cases with me.

My shoulder screams with the impact of the wall, and I collapse to the floor, Atalanta's armor clattering. More refugees step on my hands as I try to pull her up.

An old woman hunches beside the doorpoint like a guardian. She clasps her hands together, swaying them back and forth like she's imitating a fish in a current. I think she's mocking me, my hubris of trying to force a lock I don't know how to open. And then I realize she's giving me the key. A movement complicated enough to explain why the doorpoint went undiscovered for so long.

I lurch to standing as the space empties of the last refugees. I swing my research drone pack to my back and clutch the mind scanner case between my legs. I hoist Atalanta up into a hug and clasp my hands in front of her. The emergency supply and ration case strikes the floor. I'll have to leave it. My first time hungry.

I sway my hands as my fingertips graze the painting. Earth Standard winks out of my vision.

29

Before me, the shaded brightness of a jungle, a green so deep it's almost blue. Above me, a honey sun embroiders the canopy leaves with gold outlines, a soft hum of light. For the first time since I emerged from my forty-year time leap, I feel exuberance come from fauna and flora and not the grit and grease and metallic shine of buildings and drones and inventions and human waste. I remember that feeling from the old days when the institute would be the first to walk into a new world, and the giddy joy that overtook us after, me and the other agents who had stepped through the doorpoint. Like gods descended to an alien landscape about to reap magic. Except this time it's just me and every memory broken and forgotten that accompanies.

Then my eyes adjust to the light. There's already trash among the long-armed tree roots elbowing from the ground: silvery MRE packaging frayed and dirty like decomposing leaves, small white flecks of ragged paper products, plastic of various shapes crumpled or bagged, tucked under leaves. Underneath the rich rot and life smell of the jungle, the sooty stench remnant of trash and human waste burnings rises.

I lay Atalanta down at my feet to continue her startup. *Please,* I beg the world. But I'm not sure why I'm here, what I need from it. An escape from grief maybe. A way out from what we've done to so many worlds, to each other. A way to ignore the imperative of human hunger— the belly, the heart. *To stop. Please let me stop.* But this world does not answer me beyond the insects and birds calling to each other through the trees.

I spin around to get my bearings. Behind me where I came through the doorpoint looms a stone-carved Taino zemi: a crouching, emaciated female figure with an over-large head, the mouth gaping, eyes wide and crying. Hu-Rakan, the god of hurricanes. Instead of grasping her knees like most zemis of Hu-Rakan I've found in my digs, this one's arms curve, one up, one down, like the winds of a cyclone. A strange mashup: those are Guabancex's arms, the fierce and destructive avatar of Atabey, the mother goddess of all. Here, instead of her usual rage, she weeps. With one swipe of a cyclone arm, she can wreak enough destruction to wipe out entire caciques. Both eyes look like they were inlaid with a different material that has long since fallen out. Her blank eyes will never see what has become of her people: dead from slavery, Spanish diseases, and genocide, a destruction that not even she can rival. If I let corporate reach this pocket world, she too will be erased, this monument gobbled up. I want to kneel at her feet and weep with her, worship what has been lost.

Instead, I throw a handful of small research drones from their case up into the jungle air. I keep the last one in my palm, extend my hand to the doorpoint, and let it fly from me. I send it a series of commands in its protocol language. *Go through the doorpoint. Scramble the lock. Send only messages from Divya or Isandro back.* It might be able to keep the PW closed for a few more minutes on the other side before corporate is able to decrypt the mess it will make of fluid dynamics and physics at the doorpoint threshold. But here relative, it might buy me a few more hours.

And then I do kneel in front of the zemi. Head to the forest ground, my arms splayed out. How do I speak to her? Bartolemé de las Casas wrote in his journal that the Taino behiques used cohoba smoke to hallucinate, to commune with the gods and the dead. They would starve, enter the cohoba trance, then come out with knowledge only the future or a sea of souls could know. Did they see what was coming for them on Spanish ships? I close my eyes, ready to hear the weeping of the god, ready to hear her voice, ready to be drowned. What is left for me, the last of the gleaming progeny of the institute? What is left for our golden hopes but to smash them on the rocks of this stone-faced, weeping god?

A chorus answers me. Hutia cheeps, the whistling call of peewees, palmchats' chirps, and hoots of Zenaida doves. The deep caw of parrots. The buzz and creak and screams of cicadas, lovelorn crickets, and assassin bugs.

Years ago, Marlena closed my eyes and taught me to identify what was living by their sound. Is this the weeping of the living world? I feel myself emptying. I try and try and try to be empty.

Then the wind of drone rotors flutters on my face. I open my eyes. My drones whir in front of me, returning to roost.

The drones project stats and maps in neon lines between the trees. This world is long-time by the order of twenty, every day here just over an hour standard. A small world, less than ten acres of jungle. A small stream. A circle of Taino archaeological ruins threads the trees, the hybrid zemi of Hu-Rakan and Guabancex at the center. No human life signs. If there are any Tainos here, those who carved the zemis or who might have escaped here, they must be long dead, only fossils from eons relative ago. Oxygen rate is higher than Earth Standard: the trees without humans to tumble them, only smaller animals proliferating without predators. The recent waste fires set here as modern Dominicans were evacuating would have blared incandescently bright in the oxygen.

I hold out the drones' base, let them dock. Their information maps blink out, and in their place a red macaw struts with lustrous blue-tipped wings and a yellow smear on its head like the dripping of a yolk. I recognize the Cuban macaw from Marlena's diagrams and lessons, extinct from humans hunting, capturing, and deforesting in the 1800s, which here was over a millennium relative ago. It cocks its head, trains one black eye on me. I step closer to this relic, and it startles into flight, the long red wingspan disappearing into the trees. I imagine the parrot's ancestor arriving here on the shoulder of a Taino cacique, witness first to this new land of hopes and then to the end of them.

So many ways it might have gone. Conquistadors following the Tainos inside, dragging them out to work on the plantations. The blight of Spanish disease hitching a ride on the refugees who escaped them. Or maybe they had truly escaped for a while, thrived on this tiny parcel. Maybe they lived for hundreds of years, thousands of years off this small land, but eventually, violence or a new disease or hunger or ambition killed them. Or maybe they eventually re-emerged into standard. Maybe the Tainos had never disappeared, just retreated for long enough for slavery to turn into poverty, and then re-entered, unnoticed, into Santo Domingo. Maybe I've already passed a living Taino foot, sticking out of a PW only big enough for a mat and a growling belly. I always hoped that the Tainos had escaped into a pocket world, and here I've come to yet another of their graves.

I am desperate to know for sure—what happened after their world ended. How they moved on. How they tried to live. How it all fell apart. Did they have enough time to grieve, centuries of grief, or did it happen before they realized: one step into a PW, and everything they knew evaporated? There I go, wanting something again, wanting to know.

"Buenas, Mami," Atalanta says behind me. She rises on four legs, alert.

I try not to shout with relief and risk alarming the robot programming into taking her consciousness again. Yes, I can give her time here in this PW to remain a child. I say, "Do you want to help me save something?"

She leaps up into the air, a metallic arc of elation. *Saving something.* It isn't a lie yet. Maybe what I find here before the corporates can decimate it will be enough to renew funding, to turn the tide of the institute's fall. But the institute is just another center of greed according to Delatonio. So what will that save? My life, maybe, according to me. My dreams of rebuilding everything we have destroyed. A body for Atalanta that would feel like the one she lost.

Together, we pick through the selva away from the zemi. A drone leads us. The brush flares so thick with orchids, cassava, and the succulent threads of Bayahibe roses that it's almost impassable, but these weeks relative of desperate people invading the PW have tamped down skinny paths. Just yesterday standard, this world would have been as impassable as a shroud. I step over a small stream that cuts through the selva like a scythe. A steady cacophony from the jungle warns us back. But I will not go back. There's nothing left for me back in standard but sorrow.

30

Something about the selva we pass through reminds me of the meadow world around my neck, like it's the same terrain thousands of years wilder, the shrubs and saplings now trees grown lush and tall. I even spot a patch of flower undergrowth that looks just like the dusk-blooming plant Marlena obsessed over.

Atalanta's crunching steps follow me as the path opens to a small clearing at the bottom of a hill. A stone zemi is carved into the side of the hill like a cave mouth pursed closed. Trash and ashes blow around it where someone erected and then abandoned a campsite. At the top of the hill a copse of cojobaná blocks out the sun with their many braids of tiny leaves. (*Anadenanthera peregrina*. Marlena would have specified the species if she was there.)

I recognize the hillside zemi—eyes empty like a corpse, lips laughing—as Maquetaurie Guayaba, the lord that guarded the living from the dead. Or, in some interpretations, the dead from the living. The Tainos believed death was just a passing through to another state, a transformation. They believed in the afterlife, a rewarding of good. This zemi, then, guarded that new world of good, assisted in the transformation to the afterlife.

But now a small bundle holds my attention at the base of the zemi, what I confused for a piece of trash. A young girl crouching, covered in white paint markings against her brown skin, shoulder-length black hair a cap of night. I still can't shake the feeling that this is the same world as the meadow PW, that this girl is sitting in the same spot where, at the base of a hill, I had dug and sent down a probe when this world was young. She doesn't move, and her unblinking eyes stare at nothing. The drone confirms no life signs.

Atalanta bounds toward her. So friendly, she's always been eager to include playmates in whatever she does. She stops when we reach her. "Mami, what's wrong with her?" she asks.

How do I explain death to her without triggering the programming changes again? I raise my finger lightly to the girl's cheek. Cold, the flesh resisting stiffly. In her mouth, she bites a small three-pointed zemi face between her teeth. Before her, a stick of cohoba still unsmoked sits in a polished coconut bowl, and a pipette for inhaling the smoke made of a giant hollow bird bone reclines expectantly across the bowl. Her eyes are open, not decomposed yet. I push her shoulders slightly, and her whole figure rocks in its rigor mortis crouch, her hands gripped around her knees.

All of it is strange. That the cohoba is in stick form instead of the usual disks I dug up. That she is posed in death like other Tainos have tended to her, but she does not yet smell of decomposition, only a sweet smokiness like fresh tobacco. How did she get here from across the eons?

I feel my pulse quicken. Could the Tainos have been alive here so recently? Could the lost be recovered? And what will it cost, this hubris of life? Maquetaurie Guayaba stands warning guard behind her.

"She's sleeping," I finally tell Atalanta. Above us, a brief wind rattles the trees from the miniature ecosystem and cohoba pods fall from their branches.

"Asleep like me?" Atalanta asks.

My heart skips a beat. "You're awake. And you're such a good helper, don't you think?"

She doesn't respond. She plays with some of the rattling, curved pods between her paws.

I sit in the dirt, pull out the scanning headset from its case I've been lugging. I've only ever used it on Atalanta, a living girl, as a proof of concept, and I hadn't yet gotten it fully working on any of the mummies inside the institute's labs before my time leap. The most I got from the mummies was static, but that was before the last iteration of the program that successfully pulled Atalanta's consciousness. In theory, my scanner should discover the palimpsest of ions on cell walls if enough is preserved, can construct a map of the electrical currents in the brain at the moment of death, uses algorithms to filter out noise and the dysregulation and final bursts when the heart stopped. Once the map is uploaded, I can restart it in simulation, query it.

I put it over the girl's hair like a crown. Queen of escape. Queen of answers to what happened to my past, our collective past. Queen of new discoveries. Queen of my redemption.

I settle in the bed of pods at the foot of the hillside carving while my scanner does its work. Maybe an hour or two. I can afford a few hours before Earth Standard catches up with me. I try to push away my puzzlement over this PW and the zemis and the girl in front of me; I might have answers soon enough.

It's still my birthday, the culmination of my thirty-eight years relative. What's even worth celebrating anymore? Out in Earth Standard, only one life devouring at the cost of another. Marlena still hasn't come out again, her finding peace at the cost of mine. A leaden anger weighs me down as I sit in the leaves, trying again not to want anything next, just to be here with my daughter playing in the selva underbrush, bounding up the hill and then sliding down again.

The sky softens into the slanted light of late afternoon. Atalanta lays her head in my lap, and I stroke the cool metal, remembering how she used to have the ability to spend whole days like this when she was sick, just soaking up our love as we smoothed her curly hair back, over and over until it frizzed up in every direction and she smiled again.

Atalanta swats at a pile of cohoba pods and then rises from my lap to jump in them. The animals and bugs shriek and rustle and call around us, joining in her frenzy. I listen to the chorus and wait.

31

As if I've been able to summon her, finally, I feel ice at my neck, and then Marlena materializes in front of me with her hands behind her back, blinking at the trashed jungle, then the zemi.

"Has it happened again? A short-time PW? When are we?" she asks. "Not that any time matters anymore."

I close my fists at her disregard for how long it's been since she came out, what time it is for *me*, relative. "It's complicated," I say. "We're actually in long-time. I'm . . . in trouble."

She looks around. Cocks her head at the dead Taino crowned with my scanner, and then again at a toucan dancing in the trees. Atalanta trots up to her and lovingly slams her head into Marlena's legs, almost knocking her off her feet.

"Please," I say.

Marlena takes a deep breath, composes herself. "Hello, chiquita," she says, putting her hand tentatively on the robot dog's back. "I'm not going to start a fight today," Marlena says to me. "Happy birthday."

"But what if *I* want to start a fight?" I say, my fists balled.

How could she have left me alone with this?

"What do you have, Mamá?" Atalanta noses at something behind Marlena's back.

She pulls out a bundle of flowers from a bag behind her back, thrusts them at me like she's sorry she brought them. When I look closer, Atalanta's lost first face smiles from the center of each flower. Modified Sapien Simia orchids she must have cultivated specifically for me.

"Mamá, they're beautiful!" Atalanta says, bounding around her legs.

"A memorial to her?" I say. I cross my arms. "You've cut them. They'll die."

She nods and raises her eyebrows at me. "That's the point."

She has lines around her eyes I didn't notice the last time I saw her. They still smolder like coals, her mouth in a conciliatory half smile that a year ago would have made me run to her. I want to grab her shoulders, bury myself in her, but I stay where I am. I barely remember the last time we slept together, an occasion so common then and sure to repeat that I hadn't thought to inscribe the moment in memory. It has only been a few weeks for her. Is that enough time to let go? Is one year? To think that time slowing down once brought me so much joy.

"What did you wish for?" she asks, holding the flowers awkwardly, but she also does not come closer to me.

I laugh. A vision of me earlier that morning in our old

kitchen. A candle flickering over a mango. The desire for something impossible that would cost me nothing but time: the way it used to be. I settle on saying, "I was waiting for you."

"Well. I'm here." She sits down on the jungle floor, putting her old institute bag in front of her, spreading the flowers where Atalanta can nose them in delight. She lifts out a box of the leftover cake from my previous birthday. We'd left it in Divya's PW fridge in the breakroom. An incongruous apparition in this roiling jungle, still as fresh as the day it was made.

I wince. Food has often been a trigger for Atalanta, the realization that she couldn't eat spurring awareness of what she is and her hacking of the sandboxing delimiters in her code.

"Don't worry, Mami," Atalanta says. "It's your day."

My daughter, either kind or obedient or too aware. This will be another day I reset her. Why can't I ever give her a perfect day where she makes it all the way to nighttime and I can lay her asleep still a child? I put the thought aside.

"Do you want to make a birthday wish?" Marlena asks, but we have no candles.

I reach for the stick of cohoba in front of the dead Taino girl, feel her staring eyes watching me. I strike an emergency match from Marlena's bag and touch it to the stick until a flame sprouts.

What to wish for that is still possible? Corporate is coming; the machine abolitionists right behind them. If this is a last stand, I'm not sure what I'm doing with it, what I'm doing by running my scanner on the girl. We know so little about these people, not even what they called themselves. *Taino* is just a bastardization of *nataino,* a term they used for their noblemen, not their whole people. And yet inside me glows that same ember from the early days of the institute, like what I discover here can save us.

The three of us plus the dead girl in a circle, Marlena and I sitting cross-legged, Atalanta's head on her paws. Marlena's palms cup the air, and my skin longs for her touch. The stick bright in my hands as I push it into the cake. The behiques used the smoke to walk among the dead. *Yes,* I think, *I'll walk among the dead.*

My wish: *Take me with you,* I beg first the Taino girl, then my own daughter.

I blow. After the flame, the ember gets brighter like a warning that my hopes have always been able to burn through a world, that my desires have always consumed. I fan the smoke toward my face, inhale deeply.

"Hooray!" Atalanta shouts, every birthday a cause for celebration to her.

I hold the cohoba stick out to Marlena. "Don't let me go alone this time," I say.

"Are you getting high?" She shakes her head. "I thought we could have a moment together."

"That's not what this is," I say. I sneeze violently at the burn in my nostrils.

"Then what is it?" Marlena asks from impossibly far away.

Atalanta has rolled over to look at the canopy of the trees, the dilation of the sky pushing through, and begins telling Marlena about the last day she remembers, a litany Marlena hasn't heard yet.

The trees tremble above me. The zemi of Maquetaurie Guayaba standing guard over us grins wider.

"Are you going to let me in?" I say, and I'm talking to the zemi and Marlena at the same time.

"Yes," Marlena says softly. "I'm making something out of my grief. It's beautiful. You'll like it. I'm almost done. Then you can come into the PW to see." Atalanta is still talking and I can see that what she's saying is bringing Marlena close to tears.

Maquetaurie Guayaba walks toward me, stepping over the girl at his feet. I shield my eyes as he approaches.

"Don't let her see me like this," I say about Atalanta with considerable effort, forcing my mouth around the words. "Marlena, take a walk around with her. Since it's my day. Look for the dusk bloomers. They reminded me of you." I flick over a drone to show her the way.

I don't notice them leave. At this moment, this PW feels the size of the universe. The sky dims a soft pink with the too-close clouds. Maquetaurie Guayaba stands over me and plunges a knife into my chest, cutting me open. I feel my rib cage expanding to contain both my life and my death so I can cross the threshold with Maquetaurie Guayaba as he cuts away my ruin.

32

It's my life pouring out of me, a howl like wind sluicing through the trees while it happens. I am cut in half, and the two pieces fall away, one to the right, one to the left.

Maquetaurie Guayaba's large eyes examine me. He gestures to his left, where the girl crouches, where the dead lay, where time and memory and every moment past is guarded over by his hand. The glory days of the institute, discovery-limned, scientific accolades and citations as evidence of the good we were doing, my team on each engagement a chosen family around me. The me that, while everything I touched crumbled, thought it was becoming gold. Marlena and I on a cliff strung with mermaid song, imagining our future child. Our little girl before she was exploded by a bomb. A war that sucked a world into itself. The me that imagined communing with the dead, querying them for answers. A litany of *Who did you save?* A day at the beach in Boca Chica before it was carpeted in trash, Atalanta squinting into the sun, torso submerged in waves, saying, *Look, Mamá, Mami, I'm so happy,* and I, cupping my hands to splash her in rainbow arcs, thought like a fool, *We have so much happiness to give you.*

Yes, MG and I have much in common, both of us fallen gods. Why won't he speak to me?

He gestures to his right. There are the living. The path Marlena and Atalanta must have walked down, cutting an iris through the trees. The robot dog who has my daughter's memories and knows more than my daughter could ever know, whom every day I reset. Marlena whose anger has shut me out, who will not hold on to our life with me. The way back to the doorpoint, where back in standard, PWs bubble under the skin of the world like water boiling. The PW-ravaged world. The world-ravaged PWs. Time, bent and distorted, come to steal it all away. Which is the colonizer? I can't think straight.

My ears ring. A voice tells me, *Scan complete. Would you like to execute ReviveQuery on the scan?*

It's MG speaking to me finally, isn't it? I have been assessed. He'll tell me which path to follow.

I lie down in a bed of cohoba pods. "Run ReviveQuery," I say.

33

MG puts his hand on the crouching girl's right shoulder. She blinks her eyes, alive now. She stands up from her death crouch. Around her, a semicircle of palm-thatched huts sprout among the trash and pods and leaves, a whole village appearing from memory.

"How did you get inside me?" the girl says. My headlink translates her language into Spanish in impressionistic meanings.

Of course it's a continuation of MG's examination. What brought me here, what sent me inside—there are so many places to start in time's march of tragedy. I hesitate. I settle on "I needed more."

"There's more than enough," she says. She and MG speak together with the same voice.

"There's not enough!" I shout. "I can't even keep what's mine."

She shakes her head, her jet bob and bangs swiveling around her. There's pity in her face. "You expect the world to open for you. We walk into the open world."

"I don't understand," I say. "What's the difference?"

She says with patience, "We were birthed out of a

mountain like Atabey's womb was a new world."

The high is wearing off and I realize this is not MG, but my program reconstructing her consciousness. It's garbled, or maybe this is exactly what she would have said.

I ask, "Do you mean this pocket world? Is this the womb?" I gesture around me desperately. "Or that you are from somewhere else? Is Earth not the original world? Where did you escape to?"

She smiles, aggressive like the baring of teeth or the hysterical face of MG. She steps forward from the semicircle of huts. I can feel her consciousness probing mine, brushing my memories, searching the boundaries of the program that keeps her shape, like Atalanta does to her sandboxing every time. What will she find of me? Me, child of conquistadors, daughter of a ruined world?

"Quiet," she says. She turns away. "I am not for you."

Scan corrupted, my headlink warns.

Her figure deletes from the landscape before me, my headlink hissing and warbling with static. She is self-demolishing her brain scan.

I scrabble my fingers into the dirt like I can claw her back. A memory flashes into me as the corruption takes hold. A cacica, naked but for her regal naguea covering, her body painted in elaborate white, her breasts painted to look like blazing red suns. She is in the cave in Earth Standard facing hundreds of the people of her cacique. She dips her fingers in red, paints a fish on the wall marking the doorpoint. She raises her hands, and together all her people make hand motions like they are a school of fish swimming forward. One by one, each walks forward, disappears. The girl who is also me stands up from her crouch and follows the crowd in.

"But what happened after?" I cry.

And I steal another memory from her: A behique, one of the priests who opened new worlds for them to hide, is standing near the doorpoint entrance inside this PW. The freshly carved zemi behind him, crisp markings, eyes still intact. He swirls his arms like he is calling Hu-Rakan and Atabey to give new birth, to open a womb. Hundreds of their cacique pack between the trees, powering skinny windmills made of palm fronds and turning cranks. They are creating a hurricane inside this PW's tender biosphere. The behique holds a guanín amulet that looks familiar. I feel my arms, the girl's arms, swirling around and around with the crank of the windmill she holds up in the air. The behique touches the amulet to one of the eyes of the zemi of Guabancex. Her guanín eyes have spirals as irises. The amulet's physics, sucking pressure from this world, becomes a barometric engine, the resulting hurricane so strong people have to claw their way down the path. They are moving to the doorpoint to the new world on the hillside where Maquetaurie Guayaba waits. One by one they drop their windmills and disappear into the storm away from me.

One last memory as her consciousness rips away. She

sits in the forest of a new world, holding a trembling hutia to her chest, its soft down expanding with its breath. She is afraid. She has been chosen to assist the behiques to try to close the doorpoint behind them in their latest attempt. She is to be a world eater. If it works, she will be left behind. She still remembers the grip of a conquistador's fingers on the back of her neck. Arms embrace her from behind, but she knows it is her sister by the way the fingers thread gently in hers. She will not be soft-hearted, like her fool of a friend who escaped back into the old world populated by strange conquistadors to leave the amulet for any of their people left behind to follow. She doesn't think there will be anyone left to follow them. She stands up into the light of an alien, red sun. She will be the world eater.

The memory is yanked away. "You!" she says like a slap in my mind, and then all of her is gone and she and I are no longer the same.

I am left shivering on the carpet of cohoba pods, and Atabey visits me. *World eater, world eater,* she murmurs to me with her giant curving arms. It's an accusation and not the triumphant thing the girl was preparing to be. I am filled with shame, and I roll around on the forest floor to get away from her judgment.

I try to make sense of what I've seen through my inebriation. The Taino found a new world, one with its own sun. A new universe. Our original world? Or did they create it? Of course fluid dynamics could unlock doors. We use drones to do it, but had the Taino instead harnessed hurricanes with simple manual windmills? I'm talking out loud, my thoughts ringing in my ears. Do I need the amulet I saw in the memories to access their new world? Can we replicate it with drones? And why does the girl look so recently dead, considering that she remembers conquistadors, and that this PW's time flowed so fast? Perhaps their new world was short-time. All these thousands of years and they've perhaps only experienced a year relative. But how much of what I saw was a hallucination, my own desperation?

My headlink beeps at me. Two messages, with Divya and Isandro's signatures. *Coming,* says Isandro's simply. The other is a video not yet fully compiled from slow time to mine relative. *Play,* I request. Divya and Isandro are together, a Tiny Transport hovering behind them. They are picking their way between people running away from the cave on the beach. Corporate machines and protesters roar in a furious wave after them. *Yyyyyyyyyyyyyyyooooooou-uuu* is the low drone their mouths make in the first few moments of the video, their mouths pinched and open, an accusation that echoes the Taino girl's. But they are still running to me. I'll have to wait for the rest of the message to send and compile.

When the forest stops speaking to me and I can finally sit up, a man squats beside the pile of cohoba pods I've rolled out of, watching me.

Delatonio.

34

I get on my hands and knees to vomit. I scurry away from him.

He doesn't move, stays crouched in his suit like he has all the time in the world. "Look at you. Look at what the glorious agent has come to. You still think you have the right to take anything we have, don't you?"

I grimace at him, taste bile. "I thought I had more time," I say. He must have been closer behind than I thought.

"You've been saying some interesting things," he says. He stands up and his guayabera stretches open at the neck. The guanín spiral amulet that caused us so much sorrow falls out, strung through with a brown leather cord.

Delatonio's guanín PW. One of the lost eyes of Gua-bancex. Suddenly the Taino girl's memory of someone who had escaped to standard to leave a key behind for their descendants to follow makes sense. So Delatonio stumbled on the lost key as a child. "You don't know what you have," I say.

He laughs. "Neither did that warehouse. They didn't even check a six-year-old's pocket as he left, never even noticed it was gone." He shrugs. "So. Universe Two. And this is one of the keys."

I remember his young face when I tried to take it away from him, the defiance. Which of us has the right to the key? Both of us are descendants of Tainos, but also of conquistadors, of slaves, of Arabs, of Jews fleeing the Inquisition. Which of us has the right to enter the Tainos' new world? But it won't just be entering; I know that now. Our hunger eventually gives us away. It's eating, taking, using what we find. Still, can't it save us?

I know he'll never give it to me; I know I can't ask for it.

He points to the zemi and the girl still crowned by my scanner. "Gatekeepers or guides?"

The girl deleted her scan, but the scanner can make another. And so can Delatonio if he gets my scanner. So can every corporate who stumbles on it. My last stand and all I've done is lead them to the most precious thing left to ruin.

In my hands, though, maybe this can save the institute. The grants that could come, the research. A new world with the space for all of us who are hungry, the institute and not the corporates in charge of how we flow into it according to all our best knowledge about bio-conservation, all our scholars weighing in on the ways that we could approach the Tainos with the least harm. We could send their own descendants out to greet them.

I scramble to the scanner, put the crown on my own

head as a way of keeping hold of it, dizzy as I am, wanting to collapse. The trees stop dancing for me.

I hear crashing through the underbrush, and I tense. But it is Atalanta returning, dashing between leaves that reach for her, glinting red from the setting sun. Marlena follows, winded.

"Mami!" Atalanta shouts, her robot voice modulating at a tolerable decibel. As a human, those shrieks brought ear-splitting pain along with their rapture. "We found something."

"Mami?" Delatonio whispers to himself. He looks at Atalanta with pity.

"You aren't the only one who lost," I spit at him.

"Yes," he says, still pensive and staring at her, "I'm sorry."

"What's going on?" Marlena asks.

"This is Delatonio," I say, waving my hand limply, still recovering from my nausea.

"The boy?" She processes his relative age. They eye each other like they are looking across a great, impassable distance of memory and difference. He softens, though, looking at her. Maybe it's that he's never met her and can't yet blame her, maybe that her botanist heart is apparent, the difference between us: that she thinks of life and creation, whereas I record and exhume death and knowledge. Out of the two of us, he would hate me more.

"And what does Delatonio want?" Marlena asks me.

Delatonio swings his arm, indicating the girl, the zemi of MG, the whole PW. Both the girl and MG are close-lipped and keep their thoughts to themselves. Then he holds his hands out to me, like I could save him this time. Yes, he looks like a little boy again.

"I found where the Tainos went." I sway, and Marlena and Atalanta rush to my side. I put my hands on Atalanta's back to steady myself. I turn to Delatonio. "No," I say in my defense.

He *tsk*s derisively. "Just like the first time we met, except now you're on the losing side. The companies are coming. I'm just the vanguard."

"This is *my* research, my invention." I tap the crown on my head.

"*Mine, mine, mine,*" he taunts. "*I* worked for this. I came from *nothing*. Do you know what I had to do to get to my position?"

He looks down to Atalanta at my hip. "I was once like you, little one. Don't you want to wake up?"

"She's awake," I snarl. Marlena slips her hand into mine, squeezes.

"The riot was right behind me, you know," Delatonio says. "If you hand me that scanner, we can protect her."

I stay put. My last stand. Everything most precious. But I don't see a way out of this. All the brilliant minds in the world, and now the institute is up to a single fallen agent, powerless to stop what we set in motion.

Delatonio walks toward Atalanta. "Can't you see more than you ever could?" he asks softly. He pulls out one of the saplings at his feet by the roots, shakes it at her.

"Stop," I plead.

"Chemical composition, please," he says.

"Mamá? Mami?" she whimpers.

Then Atalanta freezes in a way I've seen before, every day right before I reset her. She is jumping over the limits of her sandboxing, reordering her computational stack, accessing the intelligence of the machine, the subroutines previously forbidden her, fusing it to her self that had been a curious child, full of love and wonder.

She opens her mouth and barks off the analysis of the plant's composition. Her voice is no longer Atalanta's.

My chest heaves with a wail, and Marlena leans under me to pick up my sagging weight. "What gives you the right?" I demand.

Delatonio whirls around. "Coming from you? These worlds were meant for *me.*" He jabs his finger into the middle of his chest.

I drop Marlena's hand to reach for Atalanta, for that spot under her chin that would make this all go away, but he steps in front of me.

"Don't reset me again," Atalanta says, her voice again my little girl, but with all the memory of the times I've erased her.

Now Delatonio is close enough to pluck the crown

from my head if he wants.

Ignoring him, Marlena whispers to me, "Don't you want to know what we found?"

Yes, my wife, who has jumped back into my relative stream of time to save me. She knows me so well. I will always want to discover what there is to be found. World eater, the Taino girl had called herself, but I know that title is more fitting for me.

I pull the crown from my head. For a moment, I hold it, my crown of memory. Then I crush it in my fists, the sharp edges of the delicate sensors and imagers cutting my palms. *Wipe,* I instruct it from my headlink.

Gone, all the programming I've done over the years. Gone, any scan of the Taino girl; gone, the clean image of Atalanta. No, I will not reset her again. I throw the scanner above me into the copse of cojóbana trees on the hillside. Delatonio shouts and scrabbles up MG's zemi to reach it. Marlena takes off running down an overgrown path, and Atalanta and I follow.

35

Atalanta surges ahead, leaping and bounding same as before despite the new weight of her awareness. Palm fronds and needle leaves lash our faces, clicking in the wind. Flamboyán reds drip over our heads along with trash that is caught in the branches. Cieba, cedar, and calabash grown dense block the last embers of the sun. I'll be sick if we keep running much farther, but even now I feel emptied out, like I've been fasting. My sweat pricks me with chill.

Finally, Atalanta stops ahead of us. Another small hill rises out of the trees, a small stone windmill atop it. It's crumbling, pitted from age. The contraption echoes the girl's memory of the Taino escaping into Universe Two surrounded by makeshift windmills. If fluid dynamics controls the doors to worlds, then the Tainos, worshipers of hurricanes and earth, fashioned a key to Universe Two out of this world's weather, what even our best scientists haven't been able to do with computers and drones. This marvel has stood for thousands of years relative, waiting for the survivors who would come after.

"Marlena," I say in awe. "They escaped into Universe Two."

"And this is somehow the door?"

I nod. But how to start it up? There is no churning mechanism that I can see, nowhere on the stone body that someone can start the fins of the windmill turning. I wonder about what the Taino girl had wanted to do. She had thought she would be the link to close the access from our universe forever. Was this windmill a key or a lock? "It's part of it."

"So then we destroy it," Marlena says, "before anyone else gets here." She picks up a rock crumbled from the stone pillar under the windmill. A faint breeze rises in the air.

"Wait!" I say. "Isn't there another way? Can't we be caretakers? It doesn't have to go the way it went the last time we had contact with them."

Marlena looks at Atalanta, who has the posture of a police attack dog now and tenses between us. Marlena's voice is low, pained, like she's talking to one of her plants. "Is that what you think you're doing? Caretaking? How has that gone for you?"

Atalanta growls low, looking toward the path. My beautiful little girl, gone.

I yell, "And what have you been doing? Absenting yourself? Cutting me off? You think cutting off a whole universe will help?"

Marlena pounds the rock into the windmill. A few chips fly off. But the windmill's fins begin turning in the breeze that has suddenly quickened to a swift wind and shakes the trees into a symphony of rustling.

"He's found it," Atalanta says. She projects a drone's binoculared hologram of Delatonio inserting his amulet into Guabancex's eye at the entrance into standard, the wind originating from her statue. Guabancex is somehow holding open the portal to that short-time world in the amulet, the rush of time like a low-pressure front. She is creating a hurricane, the windmills somehow a part of it.

The door to the Tainos is opening. A hurricane is coming, one without rain, a storm of worlds and time and hunger.

Compilation complete, chimes my headlink. Divya and Isandro's last message. I project the video into the air between us so Marlena can see it too, to distract her more than anything.

"You must have a good reason for asking us both to come together," Isandro says, a strained laughter in the hologram, echoing across the cave they're in.

"Yes, well, you're alive!" Divya says. "So we're guessing you found something amazing, right? Just say the word and we can send over contracts and IP dev."

"All of us together again, right?" Isandro says. "Marlena too. It will be like the old days. And I've been thinking. We can fund a body that looks just like Atalanta used to. It would even age."

"A partner in the business, yeah?" Divya says, a gleam

in her eyes. "That's what we're offering you. I promise you, you will be rich beyond your wildest dreams, if you've found what I think you've found." Her hands, as she gesticulates, are immaculate. The same hands I knew forty years ago. Surely she's been putting them in her slow-time beauty PWs. I imagine her gesticulating with stumps, her hands in other worlds.

As the video continues, the rush of people behind them approaches. Corporates sitting atop construction cranes, excavators, and 3D printers on tractor wheels, urging them forward, behind them raging protesters still holding aloft lynched machines, denizens of the beach and survivors of the refugee stampede scrambling out of their way.

The hologram ends.

"*That?*" Marlena yells over the escalating wind and the rattling of trees. "That is what you think will save us? *Partners?* They're not our friends anymore."

"The institute—" I say.

"The institute that we knew is dead."

"You're not saving anything," Atalanta says with disappointment, and a pain in my chest blooms again at hearing her say that, at the truth she came to daily and I tried to wipe from her.

"The Tainos won't survive this," Marlena says. "For people like Delatonio, there is never enough to fill the holes gouged into them. They think they deserve everything in compensation. And for people like Divya, every universe was already theirs."

The wind pushes us closer to hear each other's words, and now we crouch low and cling to each other so as not to be blown away. The birds are screaming. Marlena would know the names of each of them who called.

"The zemi of Maquetaurie Guayaba," Atalanta says. "He's guarding the door to the afterlife, right?"

I nod. "I think the doorpoint is there."

"I'm going," she says. "To warn them."

"You can't. Mi querida," I say, feeling like I've been shattered. I cling harder to her in the wind.

"I remember what you did," she says. "I've grown up, over and over, and each time I've learned. I have no needs, no hunger, no desire. I can live a thousand years. I have the memories of a little girl. Aren't I their descendant too? It has to be me who goes."

"How will knowing a war is coming help them with any kind of peace?" Marlena says.

"Not peace," Atalanta says. "A way to close the door, Mamá."

"You're not my daughter," Marlena says.

"I know. But you're still my mother. And I remember loving you both. You should be proud of what I've become."

Atalanta breaks our hold. She creeps against the storm that is raging around us, buffeting us. She will meet the lord of the underworld at his threshold. We watch her go, the memories we created, her heuristic still full of hope and wanting to save what is left of us. I remember the Taino myth of half-dog, half-god Opiyel Guobiran, the soul dog, who accompanied souls into the afterlife—except Atalanta is plunging into the afterlife without me. There goes my soul, and she's left me behind.

The jungle closes over the path after her, the trees bending and bowing to her, thrown to the ground in the storm.

Please, do better, I whisper into a gale. How to describe the pride and grief that is my daughter surpassing me, a piece of myself leaving irrevocably? If my guess is right, and the Tainos are in time so short that the original people who came through are still alive and unaged, Marlena and I will end before she can even think about returning for us. I am ripped in two, my grief and guilt and love quitting me.

36

"How can we even stop it now?" Marlena yells into my ear.

Marlena and I cling to the base of the tower. I will give anything, I realize too late, to hold on to her, even if it means giving up an entire universe. If not for Marlena, I would follow Atalanta to the Tainos and find myself battling my own daughter just to hold her again.

I marvel at the miracle that when I sob, the gale dries my face instantly.

World eater, world eater. The Taino girl's voice whispers in my head what she wanted to become, what I think I already am.

I clutch the pendant around my neck flapping in the wind, reminding me how quick and desperate I had been to protect it from swinging against Delatonio's guanín artifact those forty years ago. At the time, I had been worried about an equal and opposite world. Doorpoints to eat each other.

I startle, release the pendant. The meadow world around my neck whips around in the bluster. Why would the Tainos have bothered to tether the meadow PW to a stone artifact but not have lived in it? Why does the meadow world remind me so much of this jungle? The night bloomers, the hill, the stream. Even though there were no mature trees in the other PW, I can recognize the geography. The meadow world, this jungle world. One short-time, one long-time. Opposite time dilations, the same geography.

My headlink confirms each PW's stats: 20.3123 short-time for the meadow world, 20.3123 long-time for this one. Almost equal mass, by a few hundred kilograms, our arrival in both of them having thrown the two out of balance. That must be what the Tainos hadn't been able to get right, the balancing. Quickly, I ask my headlink to do the math: the masses of the two worlds, plus or minus each of us inside, what would need to leave with us.

I tell Marlena over the howling of the air, "We can't stop the hurricane. But I know how we can close the door to Earth Standard." *World eater.*

I compose a message, but only to Isandro. *All those years you went looking for me. I know I have no right to ask for one more thing. I'm sending you a PW doorpoint on a drone. I need you to touch the doorpoint to the one on the cave wall. Now. There's something here that if it gets out would kill the best of us. I need you to trust me. Don't tell Divya.*

I'm not lying exactly. Spanish diseases had killed many Tainos in Earth Standard. Atalanta and the Taino girl are right. We are the disease. I am the disease. I don't know how to walk out of the world like it is a womb. I recognize how desperate I am. I have so much want in me, I want to scoop out my own heart. Maybe this is how Marlena felt when she hid from me.

I yell over the wind to Marlena, "Will you let me in?" I point to the glass disk below my throat.

I don't know if she hears me at this point. The wind roars. Our hands are slipping apart.

She nods, trusting. She pushes her arm against the wind, touches the disk between my clavicles, her fingers ice cold. Then she is gone.

By the time she realizes in her short-time that I haven't immediately followed her, it will be too late for her to do anything about it.

37

The wind unmoors me, slaps me against the gale-frenzied branches and palms hissing at a fever pitch. I seize the trunk of the next cohoba I land against. I yank off the glass disk, my fingers too clumsy in the wind to be trusted. I wrench out my last two drones from my pockets, cup them in my hands with my arms wrapped around flailing branches. I knot the disk's chain around the first drone. I free the old, almost-forgotten institute badge from my pocket and pin it to the second drone. If the little machines are strong enough to fly against the hurricane force, they might make it in time. I give them their commands on my headlink, uncurl my fingers, and surrender them to the howling air.

And then I let myself go too. Hu-Rakan's arms fling me around the selva along with leaves, animals, and trash, my skin lashed and body clubbed. I gasp for air, a sharp pain in my ribs, dirt needling my eyes. And yet somehow, around and around the forest, I find myself spun close to the eye of the storm where Delatonio laughs, unbothered, just on the calm other side of the vortex behind a veil of flying detritus.

The drone with the glass disk dangling from its body pushes past him, zipping suddenly through the calm eye, touching the doorpoint back to standard. It disappears before he can stop it. My last drone, the second one, hovers on the outskirts of the eye, just a few inches above the ground, brandishing the heavy institute badge and a collection mesh bag where it is gathering a last few kilograms of rocks and trash. Just enough to balance the worlds. He hasn't noticed it yet.

I shriek my voice hoarse, distracting him. I push through the veil of whipping detritus and then tumble into the eye, suddenly without resistance.

He comes for me, arms swinging, thinking I'll try for his amulet, try to stop what he's doing. But I don't need to take his amulet.

I keep my headlink set to the video feed from the drone that has gotten through to Earth Standard. There, our future is so slow it's almost frozen. There is Isandro, just beginning to read my message, his eyes on the drone, his slow-motion blinking. Protesters so close behind him, Divya peering over his shoulder, the corporate machines blocking out the sunlight at the mouth of the tunnel. In the crowd rushing forward is Agent Alcantara, furious, come to take his errant agent back in hand. Isandro will have only seconds standard to make the choice to trust me, to choose to cut off what he thought he hungered for. Can he do it? Would I, in his place? Universes depend on it. The video feed labors over his hand reaching toward the drone, excruciatingly slow.

Delatonio's hands clasp around my neck, and we are a flurry of arms as I scratch at his face, pushing him away. He squeezes his hands over a bruise from my battering in the selva, bursting a balloon of pain. I scream. I grab a handful of rich, red earth and decomposing leaves and throw it. He releases me, clawing at his eyes.

"What are you fighting for?" I yell at him over the howling of the wind just outside our circle. It's so dark now I only see because my last drone has turned on its spotlight.

"I want . . ." he says, panting, catching his breath with his hands on his knees. In the corner of my vision, I see the drone feed: Isandro's hands around the necklace, the pendulum of the PW swinging forward to the doorpoint on the cave wall. It's too late for Delatonio to stop anything. If he stays here any longer, he'll throw off my mass calculations. And more importantly, he will be stuck here forever. I run at him, give him a shove toward Guabancex, her arms curved open to receive him. I peel off at the last moment so he doesn't pull me through.

And then he is gone. *I want, I want, I want,* his voice still ringing in my ears. My last drone flies through, taking with it a net full of the last balancing mass and my useless weight of a badge. This world is suddenly dark, barely pierced by stars from another world.

In the feed, I watch the final seconds of slow motion. Isandro's hand swinging the necklace I've worn for months, for forty years, toward the doorpoint. Delatonio's face of disbelief as he appears beside Isandro, still stumbling from my push. I see him losing his balance, his fall on the cave floor. The crowd has reached Isandro, and a baseball bat is arced above the drone, a woman with her face in an angry mash gasping as she brings it down. Divya reaches to pull back Isandro's aged hands with her perfect ones. A ballet of thwarted ravenous desires.

The doorpoints touch. The feed from the drone blinks out.

I let my breath go in a rasp. I take Delatonio's amulet out of Guabancex's eye, and fling it into the red earth while the hurricane dies around me. Silence but for bellowing and yipping and whirring, the ruin of surviving fauna. I make myself count to a hundred to be sure. My eyes adjust to the darkness.

Trembling, I extend my fingers to Guabancex's stone zemi, her hand that holds the doorpoint. If next I see my wife instead of Earth Standard, I will know I have succeeded. Otherwise, I will emerge back into standard, in the middle of that crush of people in the cave, dancing their rage so slowly in the video. I think about how in some timescales I look like a statue, movement so slow as to be imperceptible. How without time, everything is beautiful, every gasping breath disconnected from its consequence.

My fingertip connects with the pitted mark on the stone palm.

38

Marlena stands in a thicket of flowers that dip toward her in the meadow world's dusk. Hair exploding in curled tendrils from her ponytail, her face lined softly in the dimming light. She looks like a queen, queen of living things. Have we forgiven each other?

Forgive me, I beg in my head, *I am a world eater.* If only I could give back everything I have taken.

"Is it done?" she asks.

I nod. "Earth Standard's door is gone. We'll never go back." I begin to sob in the dusk of that world, in the afterglow of the setting sun. Every gasp a sharp pain in my ribs that reminds me of the consequence of life.

She's quiet, still, considering what we have forfeited. I worry that now she has no PW retreat to wear out her anger. But then she puts her arms around me. "Come see what I've done."

She leads me through a thicket of heavy-scented blooms to emerge onto a tended garden. At the center of it, where Atabey's avatar had stood in the twinned hurricane world, curls a giant tree. The trunk grows around a giant hollow, like a hand clutching an emptiness. She must have raised it from the saplings we had tended in the apartment, accelerated its growth somehow. In the hollow, I can make out an empty chair and a bed, taken from the breakroom. Nestled in the root's knees, orchids bearing Atalanta's human face sway and bob. Dusk softens the shadows. Beetles and cicadas cry as they emerge.

It looks like the house of our grief.

But then she spins me around. We are surrounded by whites, reds, oranges, the miracle plants Marlena collected and cultivated over the years. I know some of them will bear fruit every day of their maturity. Flowers, fruits, legumes. Glowing moths burst from the bushes to land on the tree house and whisper their wings over it.

She pulls me forward to the tree, identical to the petrified trees in the world that was decimated to decorate rich houses, except that this tree hasn't yet petrified. Vibrant, living, the smell of green sap intoxicating. The flap of night birds swooping down beyond my vision. We sit on a branch overlooking a patch of garden. Our front porch.

"Happy birthday," she says. Then she starts laughing softly.

"A day, a year." I lay my head on her shoulder. She lifts my face toward hers with her fingers on my cheek. She kisses me, and I try not to sob while we wrap ourselves around each other, our legs and hips, arms and breasts finding their partner hollows. Her hands in my hair, her skin on my lips, I let myself be subsumed in her scent. Like time does not exist, all of us frozen in every memory at once, our sorrow in every joy. Like wanting anything else can fall between the cracks of the moment. That's what living this second feels like.

I pull away. "If I know Divya," I say, "she'll find a way to open a new door."

"Or create Universe Three."

For the first time, that isn't for me to know. I wonder what Atalanta will find in her new universe, whether I can lay claim to any part of what she will become.

"See that?" Marlena says, pointing at our feet.

I squint against the moth light to see a thick stalk, a green flower bud closed tightly. The night flower she came in to observe. She's still waiting for it to bloom.

Acknowledgments

Thank you to my amazing agent, Michelle Brower, with whom all things are possible. To Ann VanderMeer, who has been such a champion of my work and others, and somehow believed in this novella before she'd read a word of it, who has time and again shepherded me through the roughest early drafts to see my stories blossom. To my Tordotcom team, Eli Goldman, Hannah Smoot, Jocelyn Bright, and Emily Honer. To Islenia Mil for this brilliant cover.

I could not have finished this book without my UH Underrepresented Women of Color Coalition writing group— Monique Mills, Olivia Johnson, Joyce Ogunrinde, Tshepo Chery, April Peters-Hawkins, Maria Gonzalez, Tomiko Greer, Virmarie Correa-Fernandez, Amanda Ellis, Haley Harrell—and my sophomore writing group—Katie Runde, Stacey Swann, Gwen Kirby, Susie Lo, Sarah Domet, and Katya Apekina—who steadied me every day for two hours while I wrote this. Thank you for making deadlines breeze by in the pleasure of each other's company.

To the Fulbright Program for the year I spend living in the Dominican Republic, returning to the place of so many of my childhood summers, giving me enough to write about for a lifetime.

To my colleagues at the University of Houston, especially Alex Parsons, Ann Christensen, and J. Kastely, who fought for me and my time to write, and especially the fictioneers, who supported me no matter where my interests led. Alex, you gave me the heart of this character.

Thank you to all the Peynados for cheering me on and rushing in to love on the littles while I worked. To my extended family for feeding me stories about where we came from. They sustained me.

And, always, to my love and first writing partner, Micah. That I can do all of this, create worlds, is because you are holding me up. To Sol and Ori for allowing me the space to do this while you grow.

About the Author

Micah Dean Hicks

BRENDA PEYNADO's genre-bending short story collection, *The Rock Eaters*—featuring alien arrivals, angels falling from rooftops, virtual reality, and sorrows manifesting as tumorous stones—was named one of NPR, the New York Public Library, and *Electric Literature*'s best books of the year. Her stories have won an O. Henry Prize, a Pushcart Prize, the *Chicago Tribune*'s Nelson Algren Award, and inclusion in *The Best American Science Fiction and Fantasy*. She teaches creative writing at the University of Houston.